S0-AER-191

THE CRISTA **2** CHRONICLES

Winter Thunder

Mark Littleton

HARVEST HOUSE PUBLISHERS
EUGENE, OREGON 97402

For Joni & Kelly

Winter Thunder

Copyright © 1992 by Mark Littleton
Published by Harvest House Publishers
Eugene, Oregon 97402

Library of Congress Cataloging-in-Publication Data

Littleton, Mark R., 1950–
   Winter thunder / Mark Littleton.
     p.   cm. — (The Crista chronicles series ; bk. 2)
   Summary: Although she enjoys ice skating and horseback riding with a
moody boy who has come to stay nearby with his grandparents, twelve-
year-old Christa wonders what secrets he may be hiding. Sequel to *Secrets of
Moonlight Mountain.*
   ISBN 1-56507-008-9
  [1. Emotional problems—Fiction   2. Divorce—Fiction.
3. Friendship—Fiction.   4. Christian life—Fiction.]   I. Title.
II. Series: Littleton, Mark R., 1950–   Crista chronicles series ; bk. 2.
PZ7.L7364W1   1992
[Fic]—dc20   92-5433
                                                 CIP
                                                 AC

Printed in the United States of America.

Contents

· 1 ·

New Neighbor

"It happened right down the cove, huh?" Nadine Semms asked as she watched Crista Mayfield lace up her skates.

"That's where the houses are," Crista answered. "But I don't think whoever did it would come up here, especially to a house where people are."

"Yeah, you're right," Nadine replied with a shiver, "but it kind of gives me the creeps."

Crista grinned up at her and said, "They'll catch him—they always do."

Crista tugged the laces till they were tight. The frigid air bit her cheeks as she looked over the lake with longing. It was the first skate of the season. A crisp, dry snow had fluttered down the day before, and then lashing winds had whipped the light flakes into huge drifts on the edge of the woods. But the lake itself was clear, the ice as shiny and bright as a mirror.

"Or her," Nadine added.

"Oh, it's not a her."

"Maybe it's two he's and three her's," Nadine said with a laugh.

"They'll catch them," Crista said confidently. "Anyway, I'm not going to worry about people wrecking empty houses. Ours is far from empty. It would be kind of neat to catch him though."

Crista and Nadine continued talking about a recent spate of break-ins that had occurred near Crista's cove on the lake. The houses were usually summer cottages that had been closed up for the winter. Someone had been breaking windows, climbing in, and destroying the place. Crista's father, Dr. Jason Mayfield, had read them the story from the newspaper that morning. After he finished the article he added, "They'll make a mistake soon enough and then they'll land in the slammer."

For once, Crista had agreed with her father about something. She put the worry out of her mind, even though the break-ins had occurred less than a half mile down the lake from their cabin.

"Can you do any tricks?" Nadine asked, changing the subject. Nadine had given birth to twins, a boy and girl, only a week before. She and her husband Johnny lived in a cabin on the far side of Moonlight Mountain, above Crista's lakeside home. The Semms were living with Crista and her father for the time being because Crista's father was a medical doctor and the back roads were still blocked with snow.

"Bunny hops, spins, pirouettes—not very well," Crista said. "I've tried a single axel now and then. I can go backward fairly well. But I like to feel the wind on my face."

Crista smiled up at her friend. They had met months before and, even though Nadine was 20 now and Crista was only 12, they were close friends.

"But last year," Crista continued, "Jeannie Stecher and I did a fairly decent horse on skates. She was the head and I was the rump. We did it at the Winter Carnival."

"What's that?"

"Down the lake a bit there's a big resort area," Crista explained, finishing the last knot on her scuffed, white skates. "They clear off the ice and have a big party, mostly for kids. After the main show everyone dresses up in different costumes and goes to a skate dance. It's fun."

"So are you going?" Nadine pulled her beautiful platinum hair back as the breeze threw it into her eyes.

"Oh, probably," Crista said, standing up. "But Jeannie moved away, so I don't have anyone to practice with. But this year I want to do something different— not a horse, anyway. Maybe a giraffe!" She chuckled at the thought.

"Well, I have to go up and feed Johnny Junior and Fairlight," Nadine said with a smile. "Happy skating." She squeezed Crista's shoulder and went back up the trail Johnny had dug out that morning.

Crista gazed across the lake. The ice had to be at least two feet thick. She knew it was safe all over. With freezing temperatures for the whole past month there was no chance of breaking through.

Her father had gone to the hospital that morning to make rounds. He was in general family practice now, but he had been thinking of going back into baby-doctoring since he had helped deliver Nadine's twins. Crista hoped he would, but knew she shouldn't push it.

She began walking toward the ice, still a bit wobbly. The skate laces were tight, though, and the blade protectors fit well. Because it was a man-made lake, with a dam not far from Crista's cove, the ice sometimes buckled around the edges when the authorities let more water out. As a result, a tilt of ice, broken into shards, lay around the rim.

Crista took off the skate protectors. The bright silver blades glinted in the sunlight. She stepped cautiously over the buckled ice onto the flat area beyond. A shivery scrape resounded. Little peals of thrill shot through her heart. Besides drawing and painting, Crista's great love was skating. Sometimes she imagined herself an Olympic champion performing double and triple axels like Peggy Fleming or Dorothy Hamill or Kristi Yamaguchi, her favorite Olympic champions.

Nicking the ice with the serrated front edge of her right blade, she pushed off. The wind blew her brown hair back. The sun, high in the sky at noon, beat the ice to a dark mirror. Crista closed her eyes and shot along, stretching her limbs and moving her arms in perfect unison with her body. Skating was always a happy, majestic time for her. She wondered if God Himself was looking down and smiling at all He had done.

After ten seconds of closed-eye, open striding, she swiveled around and skated backward. She cut her right skate in front of her left and swooped along in a wide circle. She hoped she would be able to spin. She hadn't done it since last year and had really only learned to do it at the end of the season. But as she picked up speed, a raw, blazing confidence filled her. She set up the spin with one final cut, then, with her left foot flung out behind her, she drew her arms in slightly, bent her knee, and began a slow, poised rotation. After placing both skates on the ice, she pulled her arms in. The spin accelerated. She opened her eyes and looked up. The clouds above suddenly seemed to be spinning around her as if she was the one who was still.

A moment later, she cut her left skate out and stopped. She felt a little dizzy. But the lightheadedness was sheer pleasure. "I love it!" she shouted, and clapped her hands.

Immediately, she darted off again. This time she skated up the cove toward the main part of the lake. Picking up speed, the wind buzzed on her face. She felt warm, but the air was frigid and seemed to cut her cheeks like hundreds of tiny needles. She swerved, turned around, skated backward, switched forward, bunny hopped, spun, and danced. It was a marvel. She laughed out loud with joy.

Moving even faster, she prepared herself for a single axel. Shifting her body to the forward position, she sped up. It would be difficult. She spotted the point where she wanted to try it. Her speed increased. She pivoted backward. She was ready. *Now!*

She leaped, twisted, came down.

"No!" she yelled with sudden pain. Her skate wasn't straight. A moment later, she was on her backside, spinning and nicking the ice with the backs of her blades. "Rats," she mumbled and pounded her pink-mittened fist on the ice. Then she stopped.

"Oh, well," she said as she got up, "can't win 'em all." Suddenly she noticed how close she was to the shore. She had already reached the last house on the street. A white dock sat on the beach, pulled up on its barrels and resting in place like a sleeping walrus. A moment later she heard a loud *shoof* and something skittered over the ice. Her eyes followed the shoreline.

There was another loud *shoof*.

"What is that?" she murmured.

Then she saw him. A boy, standing beyond one of the docks with a slingshot in his hand. "Good grief," she said aloud, catching her breath. "Is he shooting at me?"

The boy didn't pay any attention to her.

Shoof! This time she saw a BB ricochet off one of the 50-gallon barrels under the dock and bounce out over the lake.

"Hey!" she yelled. "You could hit somebody!"

Momentarily the boy stopped, stared at her, then aimed the slingshot in her direction. Crista instinctively ducked. "Hey! You could hurt someone!" she shouted again.

The boy laughed. "I don't have a BB in it."

"You still shouldn't aim that at someone," Crista said, feeling the fury build in her chest. "Any responsible person knows that."

"So you have to order me around about it," the boy answered, his eyes and lips narrowed with mock irritation. "If I were going to shoot you, I'd go like this."

He lifted the slingshot again and drew the band back.

"That's not funny," Crista shouted. "If you aim that at me one more time, I'm calling the police!"

"Yeah, well, maybe I won't lift it again." He put the slingshot down.

Fuming, Crista put her hands on her hips. "Who are you, anyway?"

"None of your business."

"You live on my street and my street *is* my business. Now who are you?"

Crista's determination must have gotten to him, because he appeared to relax and finally shrugged. "I'm staying here with my grandparents—just for a short time till my dad comes to get me."

Her anger subsiding, Crista gazed at him evenly. "Why don't you do something sensible instead of shooting a dangerous weapon like that?"

"This isn't very dangerous. Anyway, there's nothing else to do around here."

"There are plenty of things to do for people who have a brain," Crista said, shaking her head.

The boy was good-looking. She could see that even at a distance, but she didn't like him playing with the slingshot, and he wasn't shooting stones, he was shooting BBs. They could really hurt someone. "You can go skating or ice-fishing or skiing around here you know, instead of scaring everybody under the sun."

"Oh, so now you want me to go skating with you?"

Eyeing him with exasperation, Crista suddenly started to skate toward her property. "I'm not asking you to do anything with me; I'm suggesting you do something other than shoot a slingshot."

The boy watched her skate a moment, then said, "I bet you think you're a real Olympic champion, don't you?"

Crista stopped. Having just imagined that a few minutes ago, she suddenly felt a flush of embarrassment. How could he know that? But she said, "I'm just having a good time. And you're a major dope, if you ask me."

"Takes one to know one."

He started to aim the slingshot at the dock again. Crista snorted with derision and skated off into the middle of the lake and ignored him. Just what she needed, a real jerk on her street. As she cruised along, though, she noticed he had stopped shooting and was watching her. She decided to try another axel. This time she sprang properly, but her right foot caught her left ankle and she flipped onto the ice.

A moment later, she heard him laughing. "Some Olympic champion!"

Crista was on her feet in an instant. "Why don't you just shut up!"

He aimed high in the air and a second later he fired. She saw a BB land far beyond her on the ice.

"I'm calling the police!" she shouted, and was off toward her dock, her chest pulsing with fury, her mouth twisted with hot words. She knew she wasn't going to call the police, but he shouldn't be shooting a slingshot anywhere near a person. What he needed was a whale of a spanking or to go to jail or something.

· 2 ·

Race

When Crista went back to the lake a couple hours later, after lunch and a long talk with Nadine in the cabin, she peered down the shoreline for signs of the boy. She didn't see him.

"Good thing," she mumbled, feeling slightly miffed. "I don't need someone like him around here."

She got out her skates, then pulled on her backpack with her boots inside. This time Rontu and Tigger were with her. Rontu was a tall, stately milk-white Great Dane with crystal-blue eyes. Tigger was a light brown Shelty, small, with only one eye. He'd lost the other in a fight, Crista assumed, but it wasn't pretty and gave Tigger a tough-dog look. Until two weeks ago, they had been strays. But Crista's father had recently allowed her to keep them at home. So far, they had proven to be well-trained and friendly pets.

She finished lacing up the skates and headed out to the ice. "It might be okay going to the island," she said to herself, but it had to be a half mile over on the ice. The island was a large pimple of land filled with pines in the middle of the lake. It had strange dark trails over and around it. Huge rocks studded the shoreline, and at several places the rocky shelves jutted out into the water like jetties. In the summer, divers, swimmers, and picnickers were all over it. In the winter, though, it was basically deserted.

She had never gone alone before. Last year Jeannie, her friend from the next section of cabins over, had gone with her. And another time she had made the trek with her mother—the year before she was killed.

Crista warmed up on the ice in front of her property. She laid the backpack down and tried another axel, but decided, after a fall, that she would have to get someone to help her with that. Rontu and Tigger watched, wagging their tails and prancing about on the ice like they were at a party.

Then she spotted the boy sitting on the dock in front of her part of the lake. She picked up the backpack in a sudden huff and told herself to ignore him. Rontu woofed and Tigger tagged along beside her. Both of their noses were pointed in the boy's direction with interest. "Just pretend he's not even there," Crista said. She concentrated on her skating and tricks.

Her concentration was so good, that when the boy skated by her, she was stunned. He seemed to come out of nowhere. The slingshot hung from his belt. He tagged her as he went by.

"Hey!" Crista cried, as she whipped around.

"Got you. You're it," the boy shouted, and cut around to the right on a pair of shiny new hockey skates.

"I'm not letting some boy do this," Crista said with clenched teeth and was after him in a flash. Both dogs tried to run after her, but their paws slid on the ice and they couldn't make any headway.

The boy swept along the middle of the lake taunting Crista in a nasal voice. "Can't catch me. You're it. It till the day you die. Bet you can't catch me!"

Breathless, Crista wheezed, "When I get done with you, you won't know what happened."

He swerved back and forth in quick, easy strides. He was good. She realized he probably played hockey. He was fast, too. What irked her was she was going at full speed and he just seemed to be toying with her. He cut left and right, made deft swivels and sudden stops and starts that Crista recognized as typical hockey tactics. She couldn't catch him. Hockey skates, she knew, were more difficult to skate on, but also faster and more maneuverable than figure skates.

He led all the way to the other side of the lake. Speeding back and forth, in and out, along the shoreline, he kept up a steady stream of taunts. "A jellyfish is faster than you," he yelled. "My grandmother in the nursing home is faster than you. . . . All tricks and still in a fix!"

Crista's anger grew. Why was he doing this? Still, she wasn't going to let him prove her weak or slow!

She realized she had to be careful. Near the shore rocks frequently poked up through the ice, offering perfect stumbling blocks to a skater not looking where he or she was going. Trying to keep her eye on the boy and the ice at the same time, she watched for the little nubs of rock that might catch her skate.

In a few minutes, they were all the way to the end of the cove. Here and there buoys, frozen in place, sat like little islands. The boy went backward and forward around the buoys and rocks effortlessly. He was good, really good. But it only made Crista angrier. What right did he have to come in and make her day all wrong?

As she narrowed her eyes for one last sprint after him, she didn't see the jagged little vee of rock to the right of a buoy. Just as her right skate touched down, she hit it.

Boom!

She was down, tumbling, feet over her head. A second later, she crunched down, flat on her back, right on the ring of another low buoy. It cracked into her back like a bat, knocking the wind out of her. She lay flat on the ice, unable to breathe.

Trying to suck in air, nothing came.

"I . . . can't . . . breathe!" she tried to cry. But nothing came out. She felt as if her whole body had been turned inside out. Pain seared through her back. *Something had to be broken*, her mind wailed. Why, oh why had she let him taunt her? The sky above her suddenly looked huge and blue, and the burning sensation in her shoulders made her wince. Then her breath came in a great heave as her diaphragm uncoiled.

A moment later she was crying, holding her knee. "Oh, it hurts!"

A second later, he stood over her and then knelt.

"Are you okay?" His eyes, frightened but sincere, looked at her. "Are you okay?"

"No, I'm not okay!" Crista snapped, and howled again as she straightened her leg.

He put his gloved hand under her knee. "I'm sorry. I'm really sorry. Is anything broken?"

His sudden change of attitude made her forget the pain for a moment. She stretched out her foot and blinked. "No, I think everything's okay."

She sat back, her hands behind her on the ice. "Oh, my shoulder . . ."

"Let me see," he said, and touched her shoulder. "There?"

"Yeah. It's okay."

Still feeling wobbly and dizzy, she leaned forward and breathed deeply. "I'm okay, I think. I think everything's okay."

He helped her up. "I'm sorry. I know I shouldn't have done that. I'm sorry. I really am. I always end up hurting someone."

The sudden reversal amazed her. Who on earth was this kid?

She leaned forward, slowly, still wobbly. Her knee ached and her calf was shaking. After a few seconds of skating slowly around, with him still at her elbow, she felt better. She would probably ache in the morning, but nothing was permanently damaged.

"I think I'm okay now," she said, still drawing, deeply on the frigid air.

He nodded. "I always do these things; I always blow it."

Sighing and finally getting her heartbeat and breathing under control, Crista said, "Who are you, anyway?"

"Jeff. Jeff Pallaci. I'm really sorry. I really am." He didn't look as proud or cocky as before. In fact, he had one of the most repentant faces she had ever seen. His eyes were downcast and his voice almost a whimper.

"I'm Crista Mayfield. I live down at the other end of the street."

"I know."

"You know?"

"I've seen you," he said. "And your dogs. I've been up here for a week now."

By then, the two dogs had almost reached them. Rontu and Tigger each gave Jeff a hearty sniff, then followed Jeff and Crista as the pair worked their way back to Crista's beach.

"How old are you?" Crista suddenly asked.

"Twelve," he answered. "Thirteen next month." He still had that scared look, like kids always have when they have caused something terrible to happen.

"I'm 12, too." Crista smiled this time.

"Sorry about the slingshot," he said.

"It's okay—just promise you won't aim it at anyone."

"Yeah."

Jeff wore a navy-colored ski parka and a blue striped hat. For the moment Crista liked the idea of a new friend on her street, even if things hadn't started off so well. Since her cabin was a bit isolated, and most of the neighbors came to the lake only in the summer, she had no friends in her immediate neighborhood. And since Jeannie had moved, she had had no one close by. Her leg felt much better now. Suddenly she thought of something and looked at him. "Oh, by the way..."

He looked into her eyes for a moment. "What?"

"You're it." She tagged him quickly and peeled off straight for her home shore. She knew she probably couldn't beat him straight out, but maybe her head start would help.

He stared at her, dumbfounded for a second, then gleefully darted out after her. "No one does that to me!" he cried.

She yelled back, "I just did!"

She made it to the other side before he caught her—but not by much. She clattered up over the broken ice at the edge and stood on the shore. "See, I told you I could beat you!"

He stopped and skated back and forth on the ice. "All right, you win." Then he looked embarrassed and turned red. When she said nothing, he finally said, "Want to skate around for awhile?"

She shrugged. "Sure. We could go all the way to the island if you want." She wondered if he might work out as her partner in the costume contest at the Winter Carnival. He really wasn't so bad after all . . . maybe he just made a bad first impression. She decided to give him a chance. *He was better than nothing*, she told herself.

· 3 ·

The Island

"I used to play hockey," Jeff said as they skated up the shore past the houses. "I guess you figured that out." He played around, going backward one moment, forward the next. He was great on skates, she could see that. But his playful, cocky side was coming out again.

"You're pretty good," Crista answered. She was still wearing the backpack, and Jeff had picked up his own pack with his boots in it. The slingshot still hung from his belt. She had thought of asking him to leave it behind, but she decided just to let the situation drop for the time being.

The two dogs padded along behind them. "This is Rontu," she said, pointing to the Great Dane. "And that's Tigger. They're really friendly—they won't bite or anything."

"Yeah, I guess if they were going to, they would have by now." He looked at Rontu and said, "Woof!" The big dog barked in response. Jeff said, "See? We're friends."

"Right."

"So where's your home?" Crista asked, making conversation as she skated along, keeping up with him but watching the ice intently.

"Philadelphia," he answered.

"Are you up for vacation?"

"No, I'm staying for awhile."

"Are your parents here?"

"Nope. My dad's coming sometime soon, though."
The way he said it struck her as strange for a moment
because he looked away—he didn't look her in the eye
like he had been.

"Oh. So you're staying with your grandparents?"

"I guess."

"You guess?"

He shrugged. "For a little while." He spun off over
the ice, whooped, and pulled out his slingshot, firing it
into the air. When he came back to her he said, "Race
again?"

She shook her head. "No."

But as he stopped in front of her, she suddenly
yelled, "To the point!" and dug in with her blades,
again catching him off-guard. She sprinted over the
ice on the tips of her skates, then began cutting the ice
neatly in long, strong strokes. She heard him behind
her.

"No one beats me to the point!" he yelled, and
whooped again.

He was gaining on her. He passed her just before
they reached the point. He stopped with a shower of
shaved ice.

"Okay," she wheezed, bending over. "No more racing."

He smiled. "Can't be beat by a girl."

Crista snorted, but found herself liking him—even
if he was a little strange and a show-off. Still, she
wondered why he seemed so secretive about his parents. Were they divorced? Was he really just visiting?

Somehow she sensed something more was behind it all.

A hundred thoughts crackled through Crista's mind. What if his parents were movie stars and were off in France or someplace making a new movie? Still, she didn't know of any movie stars named Pallaci. What if they had gone on a vacation in Africa and were missing? What if his father was a commando who fought in a war somewhere and his mother had gone to join him for love?

She smiled at her thoughts, but was sure it had to be something much more down-to-earth. Probably his parents were just letting him have a little time away for some reason.

More questions came in rapid fire. "So are you going to go to school up here?" Crista asked.

"For awhile."

"What grade are you in?"

"Sixth."

Crista's heart jumped. "I'm in sixth grade, too," she said. They were skating faster again. In a matter of minutes they passed the second point. "You'll probably be in my class," Crista said. "There are more girls in it and it's smaller, so they will put you in there for sure. Mrs. Roberts is really nice. And we have a great art teacher, Mrs. Bevans. And it's just a really good school."

Crista was talking fast now and she wasn't even sure why. Jeff had blond hair and a cute face with a straight nose, friendly mouth, and eyebrows darker than his hair. He looked a little more grown-up than most of the boys she knew. She would have to be careful about this. He was the kind of boy all the girls would be talking about.

"Have you ever been to the island?" Crista asked, and stooped down to brush a patch of snow off Tigger's nose. The little dog licked her mittened hand and then shook himself.

"Nope," he said, looking past her to the point. "I've seen it though, in the summer. We've passed it in our boat." He looked at her with cool green eyes. He had some freckles across his nose and cheeks. His cheeks were rosy and healthy looking. He looked a little Scandinavian, although from his name Crista thought his father must be Italian.

"Who are your grandparents?" Crista asked.

"The Halperns."

"They live here year-round, don't they?"

"Yeah. He says he knows your father."

"How did you know about me?"

Jeff laughed. "I asked him at lunch." He gave her a wide-eyed, comical-clown look and then pretended he had a hockey stick and began to slap an imaginary puck around. "Pass it to ya?"

Crista knew a little about hockey, so she played opposite him, receiving the pretend puck and shooting it back.

Then Jeff was suddenly boring toward an imaginary goal, all the while keeping up a monologue. "Pallaci is alone. Pallaci is beating down on the goalie. Johannsen's the best goalie in the league, but Pallaci is the best forward. It's one-on-one. Will he make it? *Bam*! Pallaci fires. It's a crack shot, upper-left corner. Johannsen moves. His glove is up. No—it's a goal for the Flyers! The crowd is in an uproar. Pallaci and the Flyers take the Stanley Cup!"

Jeff danced on the ice, holding up his imaginary stick and shouting. Crista laughed and rolled her eyes.

Jeff skated back, grinning like a wild monkey. "I'm great, right?"

"Right."

They reached the second point and Crista remembered last summer when Mr. Halpern—Jeff's grandfather—had shown off a string of trout he had caught. Crista and her father had been driving on the road toward town when they saw Mr. Halpern, stopped, and her dad commented on the catch.

As they rounded the second point, Jeff suddenly said, "I have a dog, too." They were both skating slow enough now that Rontu and Tigger could run alongside them, their nails making ticking noises on the ice.

"What is his name?"

"It's a her. Kirstie. Kirstie, after some actress my mom likes."

"That's a nice name."

"Yeah. She's a springer spaniel." Jeff grinned again, then turned his face forward.

"How come she's not here?"

"She's with my mom."

"Oh." At that moment Crista wanted to ask him why he wasn't with his mom or his father, but she thought he might be uneasy about it.

In a few minutes, they reached the end of several points of land that jutted far out into the water. Once around this section Crista knew that they would be able to see the island. People skated all over the lake and already there were plenty of blade marks on the ice. Crista even noticed several snowmobile tracks scraped into the ice. Obviously, people had snowmobiled all over the lake, too.

She looked up and shielded her eyes from the fierce sunlight. "There it is," she said.

Straining to look, Jeff squinted into the light. "I should have worn my glasses."

"Oh, you wear glasses?"

"For long distance. I'm nearsighted. But I can see the island. It's kind of blurry, though." They continued toward the island. A line of smoke rose above the trees on the island.

"Hey! Somebody has made a fire!" Crista exclaimed. "I wonder who it is? Maybe it's bank robbers or something?" She glanced at Jeff gleefully.

"Bank robbers!" He made a machine-gun noise with his mouth. "I've got my Browning automatic rifle here—that will take care of them. Or maybe just a thirty-aught-six."

Crista knew a thirty-aught-six was the caliber of a hunting rifle because once, at the dump, Johnny Semms had explained it to her. There were twenty-twos, one of the smallest guns. Up from that were all sorts of calibers, but she remembered thirty-aught-six and thirty-five were the most common for hunting deer.

"Let's find out who they are!" Crista cried, speeding up. "It's probably just some Boy Scouts having a weinie roast."

"Maybe it's Girl Scouts," Jeff said, keeping pace with her. He seemed very different now from their first encounter that morning. Crista even wondered if he had a girlfriend. She decided she didn't need to be thinking about those kinds of things.

·4·

The Camp Fire

In five more minutes they reached the island. It was a small, wooded knot of ground about 100 yards offshore. During the summer, boaters frequently drove to the island to have picnics or just to lie in the sun on the huge jutting rocks.

The smoke rose above the trees over the center of the island. Crista knew there was a flat spot where someone had gathered rocks up at the summit and fashioned a barbecue pit. She quickly skated over the little dike of ice at the lake's edge and stepped onto the rocks.

"Come on," she said, and waved her hand exuberantly. She sat down and began untying her skates.

Jeff followed her and took off his backpack, laying it on a hump of snow. After they had both put on their boots, Crista shielded her eyes from the sun and looked up through the trees. "I can't see anyone," she said. "But it must be someone. Maybe Captain Hook and the Lost Boys or someone like that!"

Jeff said, "I've got my slingshot."

"I hope you're not really going to use it."

"You never know," he said, grinning mischievously.

They turned toward the trail, blanketed in snow but beaten down with boot tracks. They left their skates and backpacks laying on the ground. The two dogs followed them as they wound their way up the incline. As they climbed Crista noticed tracks coming in from another trail—more boot tracks. She stopped.

"Two of them?" she said.

Jeff knelt down and looked at the tracks. "Grown-ups, too, from the size of the tracks."

Looking at him with playful eyes, Crista said, "Maybe it's a witch and her humpbacked servant."

Snorting, Jeff shook his head. "You are weird. I'm supposed to be the weird one, so watch out!"

Crista chuckled, but they walked more slowly and quietly, barely daring to breathe. She wanted to see whomever it was without being seen so they could back out of a meeting if necessary.

They tiptoed slowly up the trail, their boots making little crunchy noises on the fresh snow. A moment later they heard voices. They edged around a bend and saw them—two elderly people, a man and woman. The man had a gray beard and wore a hunting cap. They were indeed roasting hot dogs over a flickering fire, obviously enjoying themselves and talking quietly.

Jeff and Crista crouched down. "They're having a picnic," he whispered. "Maybe we should just go back down."

Crista shook her head. "We can at least introduce ourselves. They were probably skating, too. Maybe they're ex-Olympic champions having a second honeymoon!"

Sighing with mock exasperation, Jeff answered, "Okay, but don't blame me if we get eaten."

They both stood. "Hello!" Crista said suddenly. She held Rontu by the collar and Jeff grabbed Tigger.

The man and woman turned in their direction.

"Hi there!" said the man, instantly smiling. "Come on in and warm yourselves by the fire. We're the only ones here today."

Crista and Jeff stepped out of the trees, still holding the dogs. "We skated up from the cove near the dam," Crista said as they proceeded into the area around the fire. "You're just out here for a picnic?"

"We were skating," said the man. He held out his hand to Jeff. "I'm Rollie Wilkins and this is my wife, Carol. We live down the lake a ways over on the other side of Route 590." After Jeff shook hands he introduced himself and Crista, then they all sat down.

"Like a hot dog?" Mr. Wilkins asked. He had rosy cheeks and a big belly. He looked a little like a young Santa Claus.

Soon they were all roasting the frankfurters over some of the coals. Crista spotted some skates hanging on a tree and a small pack at its base.

"We live down the lake a little from the cove," Mr. Wilkins explained. "Have a little farm. Don't really farm it though."

"What do you do there?" Crista asked. She sensed Jeff wasn't planning on asking questions, so she decided to plow in.

"I'm a retired newspaperman," he said. "Carol and I met about five years ago. Got married and now we're enjoying living it up a little."

He was a jolly man with a ready smile; Carol was a little on the plump side, but also friendly. Soon they were telling Crista and Jeff how they met and what it was like working for newspapers and how they loved skating. "We look forward to it every winter. Have to pray, though, that a dry snow like this comes along and that the wind will blow it all off the lake, otherwise no real skating."

As they munched their hot dogs, Carol gave one to each dog. She also brought out a big batch of potato salad, some chips, and several Kosher pickles. The fire warmed them and both Jeff and Crista took off their mittens and hats.

"Are you two long-time friends?" Mrs. Wilkins asked after everyone finished eating. She was a pretty woman, with a round face and bright brown eyes that seemed to smile at you as she talked.

"Actually, we just met today really," Crista said. "He almost killed me, but now we're getting along." She glanced at him and chuckled. "Jeff lives right down the cove from me."

After explaining about the race and Crista's fall, Mr. Wilkins jumped in with another question. "Do your parents work here at the lake or in town?"

Crista told them about her father and said her mother had died—killed in an accident over a year ago.

When Crista mentioned her father's name, Mrs. Wilkins said, "Yes, I remember reading about it. The drunk driver in town, Honey, remember?" Mr. Wilkins nodded. "We're sorry."

"It's all right," Crista said, forcing back a sudden inner tremor. "It's hard, but things seem all right." She glanced uneasily at Jeff. He was not saying much.

"How about your mom and dad?" Mrs. Wilkins asked Jeff. "I hope I'm not treading on *verboten* territory."

"I know that word—forbidden—it's German," Crista said, hoping to put Jeff more at ease. He suddenly looked intense and uncomfortable. But she wanted to hear his answer.

"I'm from a long line of Germans," Mrs. Wilkins broke in cheerily before Jeff answered. "Family background is Pennsylvania Dutch, but I'm a real black sheep in that respect." After her comment, everyone looked at Jeff and waited.

Jeff finally said, "I'm living with my grandparents right now."

There was a sudden silence. Without saying anything else, everyone seemed to realize that Jeff didn't want to be questioned any further about it. Mr. Wilkins finally said, "Want to skate with us for awhile? We're not very good, but we have fun."

Both Crista and Jeff jumped up. "Sure." The dogs barked and soon everyone headed back down the trail. For the next hour, the foursome played crack the whip and raced around the lake, between the island and the shore. After awhile, Mrs. Wilkins reluctantly informed her husband that it was time to go.

"We'll escort you back down to your place," Crista offered, giving Jeff a brief let's-do-it kind of look.

Mr. Wilkins led the way and they skated toward the shore. As they moved along, Crista studied the shoreline and the houses. Mr. Wilkins headed toward a small barn just up from the beach. He said to his wife, "I'll get them out."

"Go right ahead," Mrs. Wilkins answered.

Crista listened, wondering what they were talking about. She didn't see any car or truck in the area, so she assumed the Wilkinses had walked down the trail. But who was "them"?

Mr. Wilkins reached the beach. As he and his wife began taking off their skates and Crista was about to say goodbye, Mr. Wilkins said, "You hold on just a minute; we'll introduce you to two of our friends."

A nervous twitch shivered through Crista. *What were they going to do?* She glanced nervously at Jeff, then at the two dogs.

"Hold your dogs for a second," Mr. Wilkins said, as he stood up with his boots on.

A moment later, he opened the shed, which was more like a little barn, and immediately a horse whinnied. Seconds later, two majestic-looking horses pranced out into the cold air, whinnied, and stamped their feet. They both were covered with thick horse blankets.

"Those are your horses?" Crista said, her voice low with awe.

"Yes siree," Mr. Wilkins said with a chuckle. "I told you we're living the good life!"

The bigger horse was coal-black, a stallion, tall and powerful-looking. The other was a brown mare with a white diamond on her forehead. When they saw the dogs, both of the horses whinnied again, and laid their ears back. Mr. Wilkins quickly calmed them, "Just a couple of doggies, Thunder and Betsarama. Come and meet our friends."

He led them down to Crista and Jeff. Crista gently touched Thunder's nose with her mitten. Her fears suddenly changed to jubilant excitement. White puffs of vapor shot out from Thunder's nostrils.

"It's good to get them out in the air," Mr. Wilkins explained, "as long as you don't run them and get them too cold. We own the little stretch of land along here and use the shed to store boats and things."

Crista could see one boat inside of the shed.

"But we found we could use it for the horses, too, when we want to ride in the winter. Do either of you ride?" Mr. Wilkins looked into Crista's and Jeff's eyes and smiled. "We could use some good grooms around our lot."

Jeff quickly shook his head, but Crista said, "Once or twice. But just at a fair. Not really riding or galloping or anything."

"Well, give us a holler tomorrow or on the weekend," Mr. Wilkins said. "We'll be glad to let you ride them a bit. We can't do as much as we used to, and the horses do need to be exercised." He petted the big black horse as it stamped and snuffled in the air. "Only trouble with this one is he gets a little crazy sometimes. Once he crossed the ice in the middle of winter! There's a farm with horses on the other side of the lake, the side of your cove, I think. He's a little wild sometimes."

Crista nuzzled the horse's head. "He's so beautiful."

"Yeah, a real champ—at makin' problems," Mr. Wilkins said with a chuckle.

"Now Rollie," said Mrs. Wilkins, "you love the dear boy."

Mr. Wilkins nodded. "Yes, but one of these days if he makes too much trouble he'll end up as dog meat!" He patted the horse's mane, took off the blankets and saddled the horses, then gave Crista and Jeff directions to their house and wrote his phone number on a little slip of paper Mrs. Wilkins gave him.

"We would be glad to have you come by," she said. "Anytime."

The two adults mounted the horses and after saying goodbye headed up the trail into the woods.

Crista, Jeff, and the two dogs watched until they disappeared into the trees.

"This is fantastic!" Crista said, clapping her hands. "We can ride horses now."

"Not me," Jeff answered. He stepped back onto the ice and shifted his backpack. "Let's get home. I'm cold." He began striding back toward the cove.

"What do you mean, not you?" Crista asked, as she, Rontu, and Tigger caught up to him. Suddenly he was distant and cold, a change of mood that Crista hadn't seen before or expected.

"What's wrong?" Crista said as she kept up with him.

"I'm not riding any horse."

"Oh, it will be fun!"

"Riding horses is not fun."

"Why not?"

"Because you can fall off."

Crista shook her head. "Well, you're not supposed to do that, silly." But she could see Jeff really didn't like the idea.

"What's the matter?" she suddenly asked, as she struggled to catch up with him again. "You don't have to be in such a hurry."

"I knew I shouldn't have done this, that's all." He skated faster.

"Jeff! What's wrong?"

Calling back Jeff said, "I just have to get home." Then he slashed at the ice harder and sprinted out ahead of her.

Crista couldn't keep up and finally slowed down, breathing hard. "Now what's wrong with him?" she said to Rontu. "He's got to be the moodiest person I have ever met." Both dogs simply wagged their tails. As they watched Jeff disappear around the point, Crista sighed with frustration. "What could be wrong with riding horses?"

·5·

The Battle

The next morning, Crista skated down to Jeff's house early, hoping he wouldn't be in a bad mood again. She had her backpack packed with a snack of Fritos and a thermos full of hot chocolate. She also had some drawing pencils and a pad of paper. She hoped she might find something new to draw—maybe one of the horses. She had never drawn a real horse—only horses from pictures she had found in books.

Jeff was nowhere in sight. Rontu and Tigger sniffed through the snow on the bank as Crista stopped at Jeff's dock, took off her skates and tugged on her boots. She trekked up to the house, went inside the large open porch, and knocked on the front door. Jeff's grandmother answered.

"You're Crista," she said immediately.

Crista nodded.

"I'm Mrs. Halpern, Jeff's grandmother. Come in. He's back in his bedroom." Mrs. Halpern was tall, with white, almost silver hair pulled back into a twist. She looked "sophisticated," Crista thought, remembering her mother making the same comment. Crista hadn't noticed any car parked out front, so she thought Jeff's grandfather must have gone out. She yanked off her cap and mittens and held them in front of her, then set down the backpack inside the door.

She listened as Mrs. Halpern knocked lightly on Jeff's door. "Jeff, your friend Crista is here. Would you like her to come in?"

There was the sound of feet hitting the floor, as if he had just hopped off his bed. "Just a minute."

Moments later, Jeff appeared in the hallway. He looked at her with wide, amazed eyes.

"Just thought you might want to skate again," Crista said, glancing uneasily at Mrs. Halpern and twisting her cap and mittens in her hands.

"Yeah, I guess," Jeff said. "Come on in. Where's Rontu and Tigger?"

"Out on the porch where they'll stay," Mrs. Halpern said with a chuckle. "Sorry, but I'm not tracking up my clean floors."

"I don't mind and I don't think they do either," answered Crista.

She followed Jeff back to his room. It was a spacious, paneled room with twin beds, both made and covered with thick, shiny green quilts that looked like they were filled with goose down. On the walls were several posters, one of a basketball player, one of a hockey player and the third poster of the Philadelphia Eagles football team. She also noticed a picture of a pretty woman on one side of a hinged, gold-rimmed frame, and a picture of a man in a hunting outfit holding what looked like a shotgun in the connecting frame. One bed was covered with small green plastic soldiers, arranged in battle formation.

"I was just playing with the soldiers for awhile," Jeff said haltingly, as his grandmother waited in the doorway.

"Would you like something to drink, Crista? Jeff?" asked Jeff's grandmother.

Waiting for Jeff to answer, Crista said nothing. Then Jeff said, "Coke?" He looked at Crista and she nodded, then he added, "pretzels, too."

When Mrs. Halpern left, Crista said, "Weren't you coming out today?" She had decided not to say anything about his mood the day before, or ask why he had left without really giving her a reason.

Jeff shoved his hands into his pockets. Without his baggy ski jacket he looked tall and slim, bony. "I didn't think about it," he said.

"We could go for a hike in the woods," Crista said hopefully. She didn't feel like staying inside on a sunny winter day.

"Where to?" Jeff asked, picking up a soldier, toying with it.

"We could find out where the Wilkins' live. We don't have to go in, just take a look." Crista waited. She did want to see the Wilkins' farm and possibly look at all the horses, if there were more.

"I don't really want to ride a horse," Jeff said brusquely and plunked down on the opposite bed, still fingering the soldier.

Why did everything with him have to be like climbing a cliff? Crista wondered, feeling a twinge of anger. But she said, "We don't have to ride the horses." She definitely did not want to play with army men either. Suddenly, she realized she might be simply bothering him. "I came at the wrong time," she said suddenly. "I'll just get going."

"*No!*" Jeff jumped off the bed. "I'm sorry . . . I want to go . . . I just . . ."

Crista gazed into his green eyes. They were large and fearful-looking. If they were brown, they would remind her of Tigger's one eye—or one of the horses'. She noticed again that he often looked a little afraid— except when he was being his brash, cocky self, like he had the day before when they had met for the first time.

"We don't have to ride the horses. I'm not going to make you. I would just like to draw them."

"Okay, let's go." He tried to smile, then sighed, and took his boots out of his little closet. Everything in the room looked old to Crista, possibly antique, but she didn't think it was that old. There was a mirror over the dresser. Above the window hung a rifle. Crista didn't want to know what that was for.

When he had his boots on, they both went out—just as Mrs. Halpern showed up with the Cokes and pretzels.

"Grandmom, I'm going for a hike with Crista. Can we eat this when we get back?"

"Of course," Mrs. Halpern said. She looked relieved that Jeff was going out. Crista didn't say anything, though, and picked up her backpack by the door, then slid on her pink-and-white striped ski hat and mittens. After Jeff had his coat and gloves on they headed outside.

When they were outside, Crista said, "I left my skates down at the lake, but I can get them later. We should probably walk down by the road through the woods. It won't be as fast, but we don't know how far from the lake they are."

"Sounds all right by me," Jeff said, plodding along steadily. He seemed a little happier now that he was out in the air. Mrs. Halpern waved from the door and the two dogs pranced along, obviously happy to be off again.

Around the bend on Rock Road Crista found the little side road through the woods. It was plowed out and easy for walking. She took the Fritos out of her backpack as they shambled up the sloping drive. After opening the packet, she offered some to Jeff and he took them. She wanted to ask him why he didn't want to ride the horses, but she decided she would have to wait. It seemed to be a sensitive subject.

After they lost sight of the houses, Crista picked up a stick and rapped it against the trunks of trees. Snow showered down over them and slid down Crista's neck. "Oooh, cold!" she cried, laughing.

Jeff brushed the snow off his cap. "Don't get weird on me again, Crista." There was a strange determination in his voice that she hadn't noticed before. Already she was tired of this silent treatment. If he didn't want to be friends, all he had to do was say so.

She tapped on another tree trunk. The dogs, ahead of them on the trail, frolicked and nipped at each other. Jeff didn't say anything more.

Finally, Crista asked, "Are you mad at me or something?" She wasn't sure now how to read him at all. She rapped on another bough, and another cascade of snow plummeted over them.

"Stop it!" he yelled suddenly and glared at her fiercely.

She stopped and stared at him. "What is wrong? If you don't want to be friends, it's fine with me!"

He stared at her, then blinked his eyes and turned away. She noticed his hands were bunched into fists. He continued walking, with his shoulders hunched.

"Jeff! I don't want to make you mad, but..." She hurried after him, caught up with him and grabbed his arm. "Do you want to go back?"

"No!"

"Then what *do* you want?"

"I don't know!" He stopped and looked at his feet. His face was red with anger.

What on earth could he be so angry about? Crista battled inside herself. *All right, let him decide what to do. If he didn't want to see the horses, what did he want to do instead? Good grief, did he have to make it like she had asked him to climb Mt. Everest or something?*

Suddenly she was determined to get it out of him. "Look," she said gently, "we don't even have to see the horses or anything. We can go back and play with your army men. Whatever you want." She gazed at him, waiting for some answer. Clouds of vaporized air jetted from his lips as he breathed hard, in and out.

"I'm just mad, that's all."

"What are you mad about?"

"Everything."

She searched his eyes but he wouldn't look at her. "Well, name one thing."

He sucked in his cheeks. Rontu stood panting on his left side and looked from Crista to Jeff. Tigger nipped at something on his haunch.

"I don't even know," he finally said. "Just my parents. Being here. Everything."

"Do you want to go back?"

"No."

"Do you want to see the horses?"

He blinked. "Yes!" His face was contorted, as if a frightening inner battle was raging and his side was losing.

Crista tried to smile, but everything she thought to do felt wrong. His moods changed so quickly; she felt she had never known anyone quite like him.

"What is it, then? Are you afraid of riding a horse?"

"No."

"Then what?" This had to be the most frustrating conversation Crista had ever had.

"My mom!"

"Your mom what?" She stared at him, waiting, trying to control her breath and to make it look like her heart wasn't pounding. Now she was curious. Was this the big secret?

"My mom—just my mom." He looked away, sucking his cheek like someone had just slapped him.

"Are you upset because she isn't here?"

He closed his eyes, as if trying to shut off some horrid noise in the middle of his mind. "I don't know, I really don't know."

Crista staggered through five or six ideas about what to say or do, but she felt shut out. *What was the problem?* If he would just tell her, maybe she could help. He couldn't seem to get it out, whatever it was.

"I just don't want to go too fast," he said.

"Fast?"

"On the horses. I don't want to go fast."

"Well, neither do I, Jeff," Crista said, stamping her foot in frustration. "We don't even have to ride them at all. Good grief, do you think I'm going to make you ride or something?"

"No." He raised his eyes and finally looked at her directly. "I'm sorry. I just don't feel very good."

"About your mom?"

"Yeah, about everything."

"Is there anything you want to tell me then?"

"Yeah, I do and I don't." He looked away and sighed again. "Everything is so messed up right now."

"Well, what are you worried about? Maybe I can help somehow."

"Nobody can help."

The frustration was building in Crista again. She wanted to yell at Jeff—tell him to just spit it out, but she realized that might make it even harder. She steadied herself and forced the words to come slowly and evenly. "What is it about your mom that is making you mad?"

He looked away, up the trail. His jaw flexed and unflexed. "I'm up here because I got into trouble at home and she says she can't control me."

Crista stared at him a moment. "What did you do?"

He didn't answer.

She repeated the question and he shrugged silently. "Well," she asked, "what about your dad?"

"He's going to get me pretty soon. I think pretty soon."

"Then there's nothing to worry about."

He nodded. "Yeah, I guess so." He toed the snow, his face a picture of discouragement.

Crista gazed at him sympathetically. "I guess you feel like they don't want you around or something."

"Yeah, well, I make too much trouble for my mom, that's the real problem, I guess."

"What did you do?"

This time Jeff turned to face her, then he looked down at his feet again. "I broke a lot of windows at my school."

Staring at him with astonishment, Crista suddenly laughed nervously. "You broke the windows?"

He rolled his eyes and looked sheepish. "Yeah, about 30 of them."

"But why?"

He threw out his hands. "I don't know. I was just so mad all of a sudden. I don't know why I was, I just was."

"Well, you're not going to do it again, right?"

"Yeah, but my mom has to pay for them and she's not rich or anything, and now she's really mad and everything and . . . Now everything anybody does, she thinks I did it. Some kids started a fire behind the school and they were my friends and they said I started it when I didn't, and then everything just went wrong. I guess I just blew it, that's all." The words came in a torrent. "But when I did it—broke the windows, I mean—I felt really strong, like I could do anything, like I could make it all better, but afterward I felt . . . I don't know . . . like . . . like I always do. I don't even know what that is." He looked up at her sadly. "I guess you think I'm pretty messed up, huh?"

"Everybody's messed up," Crista said. "Come on, let's just enjoy the walk. And you don't have to worry about riding the horse either."

He nodded without enthusiasm. "I really am afraid of riding a horse."

She stopped and took a deep breath. "I don't think you're afraid of anything."

He grinned and made a sound like a horse. Instantly, the playful, cocky, I'll-show-you mood was back. "Nee-hee-hee-hee-hee."

Laughing, Crista said, "We don't have to gallop the first day, anyway. Mr. Wilkins will show us how. I mean, I've never even ridden a horse before on my own. Not like when you can really go. So what's the big deal?"

Kicking a tuft of snow, Jeff said, "Yeah, what *is* the big deal?" He howled with a strange high-pitched laugh, then grinned clownishly at her. He held out his gloved hand, "Slap it!"

Crista slapped it hard.

"That's right. Now let's go see about those galloping horses."

·6·

The Farm

They trekked down the road and finally began passing houses again. It was one cabin after another, all set back from the road. Most were shuttered up because the people who owned them only came to the lake in the summer. Crista reviewed in her mind Mr. Wilkins' directions and soon she spotted the road up to the highway. The farm should be on the other side.

On either side of the road ranged a mixture of juniper trees, thick pines with brittle, flaky brown bark, and white-and-black paper birches. Here and there a bird or squirrel skittered eerily through the quiet. Frequently Crista spotted deer tracks and pointed them out to Jeff. Twice the two dogs sniffed the tracks and ran barking off into the woods, but soon returned.

Crista adjusted her pack and pictured in her mind the drawing she wanted to do of Thunder. It would be of him galloping along, his mane and tail thrown back, his eyes fierce and set on a mark only a few yards distance. A racehorse. That was it. He was a racehorse, a thoroughbred.

Ten minutes later, they came out on the two-lane highway. Across the road was a large silver mailbox with the name *Loch Pommen Farm* written in bright red letters.

"That's it!" she cried. She held Rontu's collar as they waited to cross. The moment the last car whizzed by, the youngsters and the two dogs ran across the snow-dusted highway. The farm road was rutted, but there were fresh horseshoe tracks on the side.

"They must have been out this morning," Crista said as she stooped and looked at the tracks.

Jeff nodded. He looked more relaxed now. They walked steadily for two minutes, then came around a bend where a pile of snow cresting large gray rocks bordered the corner. Horse fences stretched back to their left. A large paddock had been cleared. A gray barn with an open hayloft stood majestically at the far end. Beyond that a white-brick farmhouse that looked fairly new sat nestled between the barn and a copse of apple trees. The horses were nowhere in sight.

"You sure they won't mind?" Jeff asked.

"They invited us," Crista answered. "They sure didn't have to."

"Yeah, I know." As they walked, he balled up clumps of snow and winged them at trees. His aim was true and most of the time he seemed to hit what he was aiming at.

"You a pitcher?"

"Last year," he said. "Little League. We won the league championship, but got beat when we played in the City Series."

"You're good," she said, watching a hurled snow-ball strike a pine tree hard. Snow sifted down from the branches. She had never been good at throwing a ball.

The two dogs trotted back and forth, sniffing here and there. Crista and Jeff passed the big, redwood-colored barn and sauntered around the driveway to the main house. Crista knocked on the door. A minute later, Mrs. Wilkins answered. She wore ski warm-up pants with a leather seat for riding, and a flannel shirt.

"We sure didn't think you'd be by already," she said with a smile. "Most people don't take us up on an invitation."

"I hope we're not here at a bad time."

"No, go on out in the barn. Rollie's out there with the horses." She pointed to the barn and called, "Rollie?"

No one answered. "Go on out, you'll find him. He's the chubby guy with the bib overalls."

Crista laughed and she and Jeff headed toward the barn. The smell of heat, hay, and horse dung stung their noses as they stepped between the open front doors. Inside stood a green tractor and several other pieces of machinery. In the back a series of stalls lined up under the hayloft. Crista counted four horse heads poking up above the rails and staring at the kids with curiosity. Thunder and Betsarama were visible in the front stalls, and a horse with a white head and mane and a gray-colored horse were behind them.

"Ho!" Mr. Wilkins called. He was forking some straw into a stall. "Come on back. Didn't expect you today!"

Giving Jeff a little jab, Crista raised her eyebrows with expectation, and both of them hurried confidently toward Mr. Wilkins. He was dressed in a flannel shirt, blue overalls, heavy brown leather boots and had a red Farmall baseball cap on his head. "You're just in time to help me muck out the stalls," he said with a grin. Handing Jeff the pitchfork, he said, "Spread out the straw. I switch the horses back and forth between both sides. Makes it easier."

Both Jeff and Crista removed their mittens and hats and laid them on a bale of hay in front of the first stall. There were eight stalls, four on each side. The four horses stood, stamping and chomping mash and hay on the left side. Thunder snorted and threw his head up and down. He seemed glad to see them. Crista hoped she would get to ride him sometime, but not at first. He still looked a little wild to her.

"This is Dollar," Mr. Wilkins said, pointing to the white horse, "and that's Lukas, the gray behind him. We named him after an author we like."

Crista smiled and reached in to pet Betsarama's nose. Jeff hung back, still holding the pitchfork.

"Did you want to try to ride them today?" Mr. Wilkins asked, as he turned to heave another bail of straw onto the floor between the rows of stalls.

Giving Jeff a quick look, Crista said, "No, we just wanted to look. I was thinking about doing a drawing."

Mr. Wilkins took the pitchfork out of Jeff's hand. "Be my guest," he said. "Do you have an easel and everything, or just a pad?"

"Just some paper and drawing pencils," Crista said.

Jeff interrupted, "I thought you wanted me to spread the straw in..."

"Just kidding," Mr. Wilkins said with a fleshy grin. "You don't think I'm gonna put you to the test the first time you're here, do you? Not unless you really want to..."

"I don't mind. I'd like to do it," Jeff replied.

"Fine then," Mr. Wilkins said.

Crista interrupted, "Is it okay for the dogs to be in here?"

"Sure," said Mr. Wilkins, momentarily cracking his knuckles. "As long as the cats don't decide to run them off." His eyes twinkled with merriment as he pointed to several multicolored cats nestled on the hay at the back of the barn.

Jeff spoke up, "I don't mind doing the stalls, really."

"They're actually just about done," Mr. Wilkins said. But he handed Jeff the pitchfork. "Just spread it out a little more evenly that's all." He looked at Crista. "Did you want to draw in here? It's not really good lighting. Or would you like to be shown around?"

He leaned back against Dollar's stall, and the white horse nuzzled his neck. Mr. Wilkins brushed the horse away with his hand. "Got to watch out for that Dollar. He'll kiss you every chance he gets."

Crista turned to Jeff, "Want to take a walk around and see everything?"

"Sure," Jeff said, finishing the stall and stepping out, rubbing his hands on his pants.

Mr. Wilkins showed them the rest of the barn, then took them back to a small chicken coop behind the house. "We like fresh eggs," he explained as he quickly walked by the roosts and checked each nest. He came up with three new eggs. The hens squawked wildly as he moved them, but they didn't fight him for the eggs. The two dogs remained outside.

"We had a problem with a little fox awhile ago," he said, "but we taught him a lesson."

Following Mr. Wilkins' nod toward the entrance, Crista and Jeff turned around. Above the door was a little fox head, perfectly preserved. Its mouth was closed and it had a repentant look on its face.

"Couldn't very well have him baring his teeth in the henhouse now, could we," Mr. Wilkins said.

Crista and Jeff laughed. Jeff pretended to aim, then fired a shot at an invisible moving fox. "Got that one!"

Smiling, Mr. Wilkins said, "There's not much here." He stepped back out into the bright light of the wintry day. "But it suits us for what we want to do. Want to come inside for a cup of hot chocolate?"

"That would be great," Crista said, again glancing at Jeff and waiting for a sign of his agreement. He arched his eyebrows with playful glee and she took that as the signal. As they walked across the yard to the back porch, they passed an old army-style Jeep.

Jeff said, "All right! GI Joe was here!"

Mr. Wilkins laughed. "It will go through almost anything. In the spring this place is a mud-pit, and in the winter, well, you can see what that's like. It's the best investment I ever made on this little farm." The seat cushions were worn away so that little but the springs and the outline of the seat were left. Crista imagined it would be fun barreling through the woods in that contraption.

Jumping aboard, Jeff bounced in the springy seat. "Now this is what I need!" he said.

"We can go for a ride later, if you want," Mr. Wilkins suggested. Jeff made gear-changing sounds and a whining brrrrrrrrr for acceleration.

"It doesn't go that fast!" Mr. Wilkins commented.

Then they both saw a Ski-Doo snowmobile parked next to the Jeep.

"Yo mama!" Jeff cried, jumping from the Jeep to the Ski-Doo. "You've got everything!"

"Yes, we're a regular amusement park here," Mr. Wilkins said, turning friendly, twinkling eyes to Crista. "Looks like Jeff is in his element," he whispered to her.

Crista nodded. "Better not give him the key, that's all."

Jeff didn't hear them; he was making loud, winding noises as if he was in a Ski-Doo race down the Matterhorn.

Behind the Ski-Doo was a blue Buick and a small, yellow Honda pickup truck. Jeff hopped off the Ski-Doo and followed them onto the porch. Everyone stamped snow off their feet and went into Mrs. Wilkins' warm kitchen.

"One coffee and two hot chocs, eating in, with sweets and moo," Mr. Wilkins announced with a grin.

"Coming up," Mrs. Wilkins replied.

Jeff said, "What was that?"

"Sugar and milk—waitress talk," Mr. Wilkins answered with a chuckle. "Carol used to be a waitress, so I like to humor her now and then." He patted his wife's arm. "She's a good one to have around. Think I should keep her?"

Both kids nodded at Mr. Wilkins' gentle ribbing. Crista could tell they really loved each other. Mrs. Wilkins served the hot chocolate and coffee in cups while the steam was still rising off them. Then she sat down and listened as Mr. Wilkins told them about how, as a kid, he had always dreamed of having his own horse and it had only come true after he had retired, sold his newspaper and business, and saved the money to buy the house at the lake.

After they finished their drinks, the two children went back outside with Mr. Wilkins. In the barn Crista started her drawing and Mr. Wilkins showed Jeff how to brush down a horse. The two dogs lay sprawled out at Crista's feet, their ears twitching. Soon they were both asleep.

Crista finished the picture in about a half hour, then she and Jeff decided to say goodbye. Mr. Wilkins made a big show of her picture to his wife, and both commented on Crista's talent. "I'm taking lessons from Freida Rutter," Crista said, "starting in January." She told him about winning a contest in the fall that offered her six months' worth of art lessons from the local artist.

"Oh, we've seen some of her work," Mrs. Wilkins exclaimed with an admiring nod. "She's very good. Quite a reputation around here."

"Her pictures are always on display," Crista said, "especially at the Roundhouse Restaurant."

"That's where I've seen them," Mrs. Wilkins added. Crista promised to finish the drawing and give it to Mrs. Wilkins to hang somewhere in her house.

"We'll have it framed," Mrs. Wilkins assured her.

Jeff suddenly piped in, "My Dad does artwork, too, but mainly he hunts."

"Really?" Mr. Wilkins said. "Where does he hunt?"

"In Alaska and Montana," Jeff said. Crista watched him with astonishment. This was the first time she had really learned anything about Jeff's family. "My grandfather—not the one here at the lake—has some trophy heads of Kodiak bear, elk, moose, black bear, and one grizzly—back when you could still hunt them. But my dad goes after geese and pheasant mainly, deer too."

"That's really something," Mr. Wilkins answered, smiling at Crista and then Jeff. "I'll have to meet him sometime."

"He'll be around," Jeff said confidently.

On the way home, Crista commented, "You and Mr. Wilkins seem to be getting to be good friends."

"I guess," Jeff said. He was holding her picture and scrutinizing it again. "You're good at drawing."

"You never said much about your dad before."

For a moment, Jeff blinked in a strange way, then quickly answered, "Guess I never thought about it."

"Oh." Crista felt a little uneasy about what Jeff had said. Something about his face, the way his voice was when he talked about his dad—there was a sense of mystery, an undertow of secretiveness—but she wasn't sure what it meant.

On the way home, Jeff played with the dogs, threw snowballs, and began taunting Crista again until he goaded her into a leg race. "To the crossing," he said, referring to the point the side road came out on Rock Road. It was a good hundred yards.

"Ready, set, go!" Jeff sprang ahead of her, but Crista dug in and it was neck and neck most of the way. Shortly before the end, Jeff spurted ahead and beat her by a good 10 feet. Both of them stopped, panted, and laughed. The dogs kept running on ahead until they turned around and saw Crista and Jeff stopped in the road.

"See, I can still beat you."

"But not by much," Crista answered. She felt exhilarated. It was good to have Jeff down the street. For all his moods, he seemed like a good person to get to know.

When they reached Jeff's house after the long trek down the road, Crista said, "Tomorrow we ride."

Jeff grinned. "I'm ready. But I get Thunder."

"I think Mr. Wilkins gets Thunder."

"Yeah. I'll take whatever." Nodding and grinning, he suddenly moved into a pretend jockey position and whipped an imaginary Thunder to the finish line. "It's Pallaci on Thunder, and Jiggins on Hot Sausage, and Little on The Doom Machine. They're coming to the post. It's neck and neck. Who will win? It's Pallaci on Thunder by a nose." Jeff threw his arms up and danced in place, then made curt bows all around.

"You are weird," Crista said.

"I know—isn't it great!" Jeff answered. "See you later, alligator." He pushed open the gate at the edge of his grandfather's parking lot.

"See you tomorrow," Crista said and yelled at Rontu and Tigger to move it. The two dogs leaped and nipped at her hand as she headed toward the lake to pick up her skates. Then she started up the street, toward home. Tomorrow they would ride, maybe even gallop.

·7·

A Chase

There was another snowstorm the next day though, and everyone was digging out. The plows still hadn't come through, so Crista didn't even have a chance to see Jeff, let alone go riding.

Then, three days later, Christmas vacation was coming to a close. Nadine and Johnny Semms had moved back up to their house with the twins. The snow had stopped long enough for everyone to plow out completely. Crista and Jeff ice-skated several times. The snow was still light, and most of the lake remained clear. Even Nadine came down one afternoon while Johnny watched the twins and skated with them. But she was still very sore from the birth of her twins.

Finally, the day before New Year's, Crista suggested that she and Jeff visit the Wilkins' farm again. "They'll wonder what happened to us," she said.

Jeff answered, "They don't expect us to come up every day." He seemed to be in one of his down moods again, so she thought she might have to laugh him out of it.

"I know, but I want to do some more drawings. Maybe I'll even do one of you—winning the race—at what is it called?"

"The Kentucky Derby?"

"Right." She smiled.

Instantly Jeff was on the imaginary horse again, singing the famous Lone Ranger theme song, "De-de-dent, de-de-dent, de-de-dent-dent-dent! De-de-dent, de-de-dent, de-de-dent-dent-dent!"

When he stopped, Crista continued, "It's nice to have a real horse so near. And maybe they'll be out in the paddock today for some running. I would really like to see how they look when they run. And we can ride, too."

Jeff agreed and they tramped up the road with Rontu and Tigger following, sniffing out squirrels and rabbits and creating mayhem. They stood at the highway, waiting to cross, when Crista suddenly heard shouting and a car horn.

Moments later, Thunder appeared on the road, careening around the bend, galloping directly toward them. The horse's hooves pounded on the road. A truck chugged down to their left and it looked like a head-on collision. But as the big horse clattered onto the highway, Crista screamed and the truck swerved out of the way.

Rontu barked and Tigger reared back. Thunder galloped across the road right in front of the four of them. They all watched, open-mouthed, as the horse pounded down the road and disappeared around a corner.

Seconds later, Mr. Wilkins sped into view in his Jeep. He stopped at the highway and yelled, "Thunder got out. Did he go down that way?"

"Yes," Crista yelled and waved him over. The two kids jumped into the Jeep. "Where's he going?"

"Probably the lake," Mr. Wilkins wheezed. "I told you there were some mares on a farm on the other side.

The horse just gets stir crazy in winter, I think. He goes down that access road at the end of your street."

"Right by Granddad's house!" Jeff said.

"Doggonit!" Mr. Wilkins yelled. "We have to move."

He cranked the gearshift and hit the gas. Crista and Jeff's heads jerked back with the motion, but both perched carefully on the springy seats. The two dogs ran along behind them. The wind whistled in her ears as they charged around the bend just in time to see Thunder take off on the road through the woods down toward the lake.

"Doggone!" shouted Mr. Wilkins above the wind. "He really is going for that lake. I should never have let him find out the way."

Crista yelled, "Will he actually cross the ice?"

"Did once," Mr. Wilkins answered. "But not usually. Usually, he just stands on the shore, pacing back and forth till I can get a halter on him. He's just loco sometimes."

The Jeep veered to the right, around the corner of the access road. They could see Thunder 100 yards ahead, his tail up, snow flying out from under his hooves. Mr. Wilkins mashed the accelerator and shards of snow spit out behind the Jeep. "He won't try it, I'm sure. It'll be the first time this winter. I don't think he'll try it."

Crista's heart hammered in her rib cage as she stared ahead trying to keep a fix on the horse. But the road dipped and she could no longer see him.

"Can either of you use a rope?"

Crista looked at Jeff. He nodded. "A little," he said, "but not a lasso."

"Don't need a lasso. Who do you think I am—Tom Mix?" Mr. Wilkins, for all his bluster, was white with anxiety.

Crista knew he referred to an old-time television cowboy even though she had never seen one of his shows.

"No way," Mr. Wilkins yelled over the wind, "I just want you to wave it at him and drive him to me."

They came over a rise, then started the descent to the lake.

"That's my house!" Jeff shouted above the wind.

Mr. Wilkins nodded, keeping his eyes on the road.

The Jeep bucked and pitched, angling back and forth and skidding in the snow. Crista could tell, though, that the Jeep had a strong grip on the rocky road.

Ten seconds later they skidded out onto the beach and stopped in a spray of snow. Thunder stood down to the right, sniffing the ice and stamping his feet. Great jets of white vaporized air huffed from his nostrils. The horse's back was wet with sweat.

"He'll get a cold if I don't get him in quick," Mr. Wilkins cried, jumping out of the Jeep. "Jeff, see if you and Crista can get over behind him. I have the halter here. You two hold either end of the rope and make like you're going to pen him in. He will probably come back toward me."

Crista grabbed the coiled rope out of the back of the Jeep and glanced at Jeff. His eyes had that daring, cocky look again and she wondered what he would do this time. She handed him one end of the rope. Jeff nodded and started after Mr. Wilkins.

"Hurry, we've got to run!" Jeff shouted.

The horse moved further up the beach so they had to pass well above him. In a minute they were on the far side. Crista ran down to the edge of the ice and Jeff stayed above her. They pulled the rope taut between them.

"All right, boy," Mr. Wilkins was saying as he moved in with the halter. "Easy now. We're not trying to scare you. Just be easy now."

He motioned to Crista and Jeff to move forward. They advanced. The two dogs stood panting behind Mr. Wilkins, watching the scene with interest. Crista called to Rontu to run up, to close the gap between them so the horse would be penned in by the dogs, the rope, the ice, and Mr. Wilkins.

Thunder snorted and stamped. The clink of the metal horseshoes on the rocks resounded, and Thunder reared up, neighing as Mr. Wilkins stepped closer. "Easy boy, don't go onto the ice. Just look at me. Gonna take you home now. You don't want to freeze out here."

The horse reared back and churned his front legs like a blind boxer. Mr. Wilkins stepped closer. Crista and Jeff held the rope tight and the two dogs advanced hesitantly but steadily in the gap. The horse was cornered.

Then Crista realized that Jeff was advancing closer and closer. She was much farther out, and a hole would open up if she didn't hurry. "Jeff, slow down!" she shouted.

Mr. Wilkins looked up. "Fill that hole!"

Crista ran in. The horse wheeled around. Nipping at the snow a moment, Thunder suddenly bolted forward right toward Jeff.

Growling like a bear, Jeff leaped at the horse's neck with the rope. He caught Thunder's neck and grabbed a tuft of mane, holding on like a deranged tick.

"Got him!" Jeff yelled. "I got him!"

Digging his heels in, the horse dragged Jeff, knocking him to his knees. Mr. Wilkins wasn't fast enough. With a whump, Jeff caught his toe on a stone. He sprawled backward as Thunder crashed by, just missing Jeff's head.

Mr. Wilkins knelt by Jeff. "You okay?"

"Yeah," Jeff said, jumping to his feet.

Mr. Wilkins shook his head. "Hey, I don't want you to kill yourself, Jeff. Now be careful. You could be trampled."

"All right," Jeff said, brushing himself off.

"Okay, then let's pin him at the edge of the woods," Mr. Wilkins shouted.

Crista and Jeff ran around the horse again carrying the rope. This time Thunder seemed to be more wary, knowing that he could not easily escape.

"Just hold the rope tight," Jeff said to Crista, taking charge. "I'll go closer if you want."

"No, I'm all right," Crista answered, steadying herself. She held the rope tight and advanced.

Thunder stood at the edge of the woods now. Mr. Wilkins had moved in to cut off any escape back toward the Jeep. The two dogs stood in the middle. Crista and Jeff ran up to cut off Thunder's flight on the other side. Again they closed in.

The horse snorted and neighed. Crista let Jeff pull her along with the rope and soon he outflanked the horse. If they could only hold their position, they might get the horse this time.

"If he gets away this time, he will go for the ice, I know it!" Mr. Wilkins yelled. "We can't let him get out there!"

Crista suddenly realized that again only Jeff stood between Thunder and freedom. Mr. Wilkins was getting closer. If the horse went for Jeff, he might trample the boy for sure. But Jeff looked unafraid. His lips were moving in a kind of prayer and he had that eager, got-to-prove-it look in his eyes again.

Thunder pawed the ground, neighing and snorting and looking from Mr. Wilkins to Jeff to Crista. Then he started forward, right at Jeff.

Crista screamed. Immediately Rontu and Tigger darted forward like two professional sheepdogs. Jeff stepped back, yelling in the horse's face. "You're not going here. Uh-uh. Not again!" This time Thunder stopped, his eyes frightened and darting about.

It was all the time Mr. Wilkins needed. A split second later, he threw the halter over Thunder's head and jerked it into place, tightening the strap and hanging on to the lead rope. Both dogs stopped barking. Crista ran to Jeff. His face was white and she saw that his knees were quivering. "That was really something," she said admiringly. "You stopped him!"

"Great job!" said Mr. Wilkins, breathing hard. His Farmall cap lay on the ground. Still holding Thunder by the lead rope, he snatched it up. "I never could have done it without you. He's a real crazy horse sometimes. You two did a real good job. Gave you a scare, though, didn't he, Jeff?"

Nodding, Jeff grinned. "I thought he was going to trample me that time."

"But you stood your ground like a man!" Mr. Wilkins smiled. "That was great!"

Mr. Wilkins tied the lead rope to the bumper of the Jeep. They drove slowly up the hill with Thunder and the dogs trotting behind. The big man led them in the singing of "The Battle Hymn of the Republic"— "What I sing after I have a little victory like this," he explained after they reached the highway, laughing and chuckling about the adventure.

After crossing the highway and getting Thunder back into the barn, Mr. Wilkins invited them in for a snack. It was past three o'clock when Crista and Jeff set out on the road to home. When they were out of sight of the farmhouse, Crista said, "Jeff, that was really crazy, leaping on the horse like that. You could have been squashed for good!"

"I know," Jeff said sheepishly. "I just...I don't know...I just had to."

"Why?"

"I felt like my dad was watching or something."

"Your dad?"

"Sometimes I feel like that."

"How come?"

"I don't know. I just feel like he's here, watching, and if I really do it right, then..." Jeff looked off into the distance and sighed, "I don't know."

"Then what?" Crista stared at him, trying to understand what went on in Jeff's mind.

"Then he'll come, I guess." Jeff looked away, then shrugged and said no more.

"Well, when is he coming up?" Crista asked. "He is coming up soon, right?"

"Yeah, soon," Jeff responded. "Maybe next weekend."

"Then I would like to meet him," Crista said with determination. "I'll tell him how brave you were."

"Would you?" Jeff looked at her with wide eyes.

"Yeah. You were really brave back there, braver than me."

"All right!" Jeff punched at the air with little jabs and made his funny, crazy, laugh sound.

Crista smiled. "Why do you do that?"

"Do what?" Jeff answered as his exuberance increased.

"Make that noise. It's strange."

"It means I'm King of the Jungle!" He leaped at her, with his clownish face and shouted, "Rrrrrrrrrr!"

"You are weird," Crista said. But she liked it.

Jeff settled down and they walked on. Jeff continued making different noises. Crista shook her head with mock unbelief. At the same time, she prayed he would be in her class at school the coming week. That would make it fun, and maybe they would even do their homework together. That would be great! She hadn't had a friend like that since Jeannie Stecher left.

·8·

Girl Talk

Nadine and Johnny came over on New Year's Day for dinner. For the first time, Crista shared her thoughts about Jeff with Nadine as they washed the dishes from their afternoon dinner of roast goose, stuffing, peas, and sweet potatoes.

"I never know if he's going to be crazy or in a bad mood or a real daredevil," Crista commented as she raked at the baked-on goose skin in the roaster. "Sometimes he acts like he doesn't even want to be friends at all."

"Maybe he just needs to be left alone for awhile—" Nadine suggested, "to make him realize what a good friend you are."

"Maybe," Crista answered. "But it was fun, and riding the horses will be great once we start doing it."

"It's really nice of Mr. and Mrs. Wilkins to let you ride them." Nadine set the last of the dishes in the drip tray and leaned on the counter. "Men can be strange sometimes, even when they are just boys like Jeff. Being tough is really important to them. You know, not crying when they are hurt, acting strong—like things never muss their feathers. Johnny's like that sometimes. And you know what it was like this fall with your dad."

67

Crista and her father had gone through over a year in a "silent spell" after the death of Crista's mother. It was hard for Crista not to talk to her father about what was going on inside each of them. The only thing that seemed to bring him out of the silence was delivering Nadine's twins. It was as if, with their life, he came back to life.

"I think this is different," Crista commented. "There's something going on with Jeff's parents. I don't know what it is. I think maybe they are getting a divorce or something."

"That's enough to throw anyone out of orbit."

"I guess. But the real problem seems to be his father. Jeff is always telling me he is coming up to get him, but he always has this strange look in his eyes when he talks about it."

Nadine sat down on a chair in the kitchen and crossed her legs. As always, she looked pretty with her long, flowing, white-blonde hair and her fabulous smile. Crista always wanted to look like her own mother, but sometimes she hoped she would be more in Nadine's style. But with her plain brown hair she definitely wasn't going to turn out to be a lightning-bolt blonde, no matter what she did. Most of the time she was just glad that Nadine was one of her best friends.

"Maybe you ought to ask Jeff's grandmother when Jeff isn't around," Nadine mused. "But then he might think you're going behind his back."

Crista thought a moment, then nodded her head. "Yeah, I don't want to make him think I'm trying to spy on him or something."

Smiling down at one of the twins in a little baby seat, Nadine said, "What else does he say about his dad?"

"That he is this big hunter." Crista pursed her mouth in thought. "Sometimes I think Jeff is trying to prove something all the time. When he grabbed Thunder around the neck, it was crazy, really crazy. He could really have been hurt. And then the way he shows off all the time. He is fun, but sometimes I think he just goes too far. And then there's the time he broke all the windows at his school." Crista told Nadine what Jeff had said about that incident. "That sort of scared me, like he really is a little crazy."

"He has a lot of built-up anger," Nadine said with a nod. "But he hasn't done anything bad since you've known him."

"No." Crista paused, thinking.

Suddenly Nadine covered her mouth and cried, "Oh, no!"

"What?"

"No, it couldn't be . . ."

"What?" Crista stared at Nadine. "What is it?"

"It's impossible. I just thought, well, didn't you tell me Jeff got here just before Christmas?"

"Yeah."

"That was when the break-ins started."

"The break-ins?" Crista gave her a puzzled look.

"Across the cove—the summer houses."

"Nadine!" Crista cried with horror, "Jeff wouldn't do that!"

Nadine nodded quickly. "You're right. Forget I ever said it."

Crista shook her head. "He's only 12 years old, Nay. He doesn't do that kind of stuff."

"I know, I know. Forget it."

With a sigh, Crista piled the last of the pots on the dripping tray and washed her hands off. She looked out the window toward the lake. The sun was just setting; Rontu and Tigger were standing on the dock watching. She didn't see anything that looked particularly interesting, but it was a pleasant, pretty scene. She thought it might be something worth capturing in her next painting.

Nonetheless, the thought was lodged in her mind. *Could Jeff be doing those break-ins? No, it was impossible. He wouldn't do something that dangerous. Never!*

"I'm not going to worry about it," Crista said with finality. "Jeff is my friend."

Nadine laughed. "Just forget the whole thing and be a good friend."

Crista smiled. "I'll do it!" she suddenly said, throwing her fist into the air.

"What are you going to do now?" a deep voice boomed as Johnny Semms came around the corner.

"Finish cleaning up this mess!" Nadine said quickly, then winked at Crista. "Girl talk, Johnny, my dear. Nothing for you to worry about."

Johnny embraced Nadine and gave her a smacking kiss. He grinned at Crista, then said, "Always did want to hear some of that 'girl talk'."

"Sorry," Crista answered. "You'll just have to become a girl if you want to get in on any of it."

Johnny shook his head. "Oh well, maybe in heaven."

Nadine patted him on the back. "Now run along, Honeybunch, Crista and I have to settle the rest of the problems in the world this afternoon before bedtime."

"Good," Johnny said, letting go, and heading back into the living room. "I was hoping that nuclear missile problem would get cleared up today. Glad to know you're going to get it wrapped up."

Shaking her head, Nadine said, "Men. Can't live with them and can't live without them."

"Right," Crista answered and both girls giggled mischievously.

• • •

After Dr. Mayfield and Johnny got a fire going in the fireplace, Nadine suggested that she and Crista take a walk down to the lake. Johnny promised to watch the twins, who were taking a nap.

Both girls bundled up and headed down the path to the lake. Rontu and Tigger bounded up to them, barking and frolicking in the snow. With the first stars coming out and a bright moon, the light shone on the ice like a dark mirror. Down the beach Crista saw a roaring fire. She was sure it was Jeff, and probably his grandfather.

"Let's go down. You can meet him," Crista said to Nadine.

They trudged through the snow toward the bonfire. It was Jeff, his grandfather, and a woman Crista didn't know. She wondered if she could be Jeff's mother.

Crista called out as she neared the fire, "Jeff, it's me—Crista."

As they stepped into the firelight, Crista introduced Nadine and told them about the recent birth of the twins. Jeff answered, "This is my grandfather and my mom, um, Jenny Pallaci." He seemed nervous again and didn't look into Crista's eyes.

Mrs. Pallaci looked stiff, wearing a heavy coat and a tam. Everyone was tightly bundled in ski parkas and warm pants and boots.

"I've heard a lot about you, Crista," Mrs. Pallaci said. "Jeff hasn't stopped talking about you." Her voice was sweet, almost sickeningly sweet, like she was talking to a toddler.

Nadine nudged Crista, but the younger girl didn't flinch. "We've been skating and stuff."

"Jeff said you rescued a horse."

Staring at Jeff across the fire, Crista said, "It wasn't just me. Jeff did most of it, and Mr. Wilkins. I just sort of stood around."

"I'm sure it was quite an experience," Mrs. Pallaci said. "You sound like a very brave girl. We all know Jeff has had his problems. Frankly, I didn't believe a word of it till now." She chuckled, but no one laughed with her.

Everyone held their mittened hands out to the fire. The saccharine gentility in Mrs. Pallaci's voice made Crista especially uneasy.

"How long are you here for?" Nadine asked, obviously changing the subject.

"I came up yesterday afternoon to see dad and mom," Mrs. Pallaci explained. "I'll be going home tomorrow."

Crista tried to catch Jeff's eyes. She noted immediately that his mother hadn't mentioned Jeff's name and it seemed like a conscious choice. Jeff still would not look up at her.

"I'm sure Jeff will fit right in at our school. We need some more boys who are good at sports and things," Crista said, thinking especially of Jeff's skating ability.

"Oh, yes, I'm sure he'll fit right in," Mrs. Pallaci said. "He always does. And hopefully, he won't get into any trouble, will you Jeffie?" She looked into Crista's eyes. "Jeff has a tendency to go off the deep end now and then, don't you?" She looked at Jeff with cold, angry eyes, but Jeff just stared at the fire. "But we're not going to have anymore of that, right?"

Jeff replied with a nod.

Mrs. Pallaci said it like she was talking to a four-year-old. Crista fought an impulse to tell the woman to stuff that kind of talk. A steeping anger began to fill her. The woman acted as if nothing was wrong—like nothing was going on, like talking that way to Jeff in front of others was perfectly normal. *Why didn't his grandfather say anything about it either? All right, Jeff made a mistake. He broke some windows. Couldn't anybody forgive him?*

When no one spoke, Mrs. Pallaci said, "Well, some of us do have work to do. I'm going back up to the house, Dad." Turning to Nadine and Crista, she said, "Nice to have met you. Keep your eye on Jeff for me, will you? Are you coming, Dad?"

Mr. Halpern grunted and started up the trail with his daughter.

Nadine nudged Crista and said, "We'd better get back, too. I'm getting a little cold."

Looking at Jeff across the fire, Crista waited for the Halperns' back door to slam. She asked, "Jeff, why do you just stand there and take that?"

He didn't answer.

"Jeff?"

The boy continued to stare at the fire.

Nadine replied, "Crista, it's time to go."

The anger twisted and ground inside of her. For the first time she felt as if she understood some of whatever Jeff was feeling, but all it did was make her angry at him for making no reply to his mother's thorny thrusts.

"Jeff, is it always like that?" she asked.

"Crista," Nadine said, grabbing her arm, "this is not the time."

"Why not?"

"Let's go, Crissie. Jeff has enough to deal with, without you making him feel worse."

Crista gazed at Jeff's downcast eyes. "Am I making you feel worse, Jeff?"

The boy's hands were shoved deep in his pockets and he kept shifting his weight nervously. His shoulders were hunched and his head bowed down.

"Jeff, please answer me."

"No, you're not making me feel worse."

"I am, aren't I?"

Nadine squeezed Crista's shoulder insistently, but Crista refused to move. She felt a thrumming inner engine pushing her to demand that Jeff say something to his mother about the situation.

With another insistent squeeze, Nadine said, "I think Jeff wants to be alone right now, Crista."

"Do you want to be alone, Jeff? Is that it?" Crista asked.

Jeff answered, "I don't know."

"What do you mean, 'I don't know'? What kind of answer is that?"

"Quit pushing it, Crista," Nadine said with clenched teeth.

"I just don't know," Jeff suddenly yelled. He stooped down, picked up a flaming stick from the fire—one end was unlit—and hurled it out onto the frozen lake. Then he turned and stomped up the trail toward the house.

"Jeff, I'm sorry!" Crista started after him, but Nadine held her back.

"Crista, you've got to let him breathe!" she cried.

With a frustrated sigh, Crista relaxed. "But it's so unfair."

"Well, imagine living with that all the time. Then you can understand Jeff a little better, right? Now come on, let's get back up to the cabin and make sure our men are happy, okay?"

Sniffling, Crista started to cry. "I didn't mean to hurt him."

Nadine hugged her. "Come on, little sister. He'll survive and so will you. Now let's get going before I lose all my toes to frostbite."

The bonfire had died down some. Crista figured that someone from the house would have the sense to put it out, so she and Nadine walked back up the beach through the light snow. They were quiet, and as the moonlight crackled off the ice, a deep determination filled her. Somehow she would be a plus in Jeff's life and not a negative. As long as he was there, she would be a plus. She set her jaw and kicked at the snow as she walked. "It's totally unfair," she mumbled, "totally."

·9·

Talk at the Dock

The next morning was the last day of vacation. Crista decided to work off some of her frustration with a long skate. She hadn't been out on the ice long when she spotted Jeff sitting on his family dock. Crista immediately skated over and stood opposite him.

"I'm sorry about last night, Jeff," she said right away. "I didn't mean to make things worse."

"It's okay," Jeff said, looking up and squinting into the sunlight. "I know you were just trying to be nice. My mom doesn't trust me. She probably never will again. It's as simple as that."

Crista took the blade protectors out of her backpack and slid them onto her ice skates. Then she stepped over the rocks to where Jeff was sitting. "Mind if I sit with you?"

Rontu and Tigger were still working their way down the lake on the beach side. They both barked when they saw Jeff help Crista climb onto the dock. Immediately in front of the dock was a long shelf of rock about three feet high, forming a wall on the beach. Crista had always wondered how the Halperns managed to pull the dock up over it. Everyone on the lake seemed to have some special contraption for hauling in docks. To change the subject, she asked, "How do you ever get this dock up over those rocks there?"

Jeff shrugged. "It's easy. See the wheels underneath the dock." He pointed to a set of old wagon wheel rims that the legs of the dock rested on. "My grandfather rigged up a winch with a cable and rope. We pull the dock up with the rope tied to a trailer ball on the back of their station wagon. When we get to the rock ledge, Grandad invented this, uh, well, let me show you."

He jumped off the dock and waited for Crista. Then he led her to a long storage box in the woods. Jeff suddenly seemed enthusiastic and full of life again. Not like the night before.

He opened the storage box and took out a steel rod with a U-shaped crown and a pulley at the bottom of the U. Jeff held it up. "We stick the rod in the sand above the ledge and lead the rope through the U at the top. It acts as a fulcrum to lift the dock up over the ledge."

"That's ingenious," Crista said. "Your grandfather invented that, huh?"

"Yeah, he has all kinds of machinery in the basement that he uses to make things. He's good at making up stuff like that."

Crista detected the pride in Jeff's voice.

"So you help him bring in the dock on Labor Day weekend?"

"Right," Jeff said. "And my uncles and their families. See," he said, picking up the winch, "we put this around this big pine tree," he pointed to a large-trunked tree at the end of the trail, "and then we just winch it right up. It's easy."

"You do all that, huh?" Crista looked from the tree to the dock and back again. It seemed like a big job to her. Bringing in her father's dock was a similar operation, but not as complex. It was more or less plain grit and muscle with no fancy contraptions.

"It's not hard at all," Jeff said. "Once you've done it about a million times like we have."

For a moment, both of them stood there, suddenly silent. Then Crista asked, "Do you want to skate again?"

"Yeah, let's. I'd really like to." Jeff smiled hesitantly, then sighed. "I'm sorry about my mom."

Crista didn't answer. Jeff was obviously uncomfortable, so she decided to wait to see what he said.

"She's just ... I don't know ..." He leaned on the storage box, crunching snow between his gloved thumb and forefinger.

"She talks to you like you're a baby."

"Yeah, well, I guess she doesn't really mean it. I mean, I hope she doesn't. But I'll be with my dad soon, so it won't be so bad." He chuckled. "Mom's okay, though. She's a lawyer and is always working, so anyway ..."

"Well, it's not right," Crista said firmly. "She shouldn't talk to you like that. You made one mistake. Everybody makes lots more than that."

Jeff brought his eyes up to Crista's. He caught her gaze a moment, then grinned and tagged her. "You're it."

He spun on his heel and sprinted up the trail. Crista couldn't run because she still had on her skates. "Get your skates!" she yelled. "I'll meet you on the ice."

They met at the lake, then skated down to the point. As always, the dogs panted along behind them, barking now and then at a bird or chipmunk that scampered down a pine branch. Crista told Jeff more about her family and her father's work. Jeff was interested and asked more questions. He didn't say anything more about his mother or father.

As they glided around the ice at the point, Crista spotted Mr. and Mrs. Wilkins again, this time standing on the ice, and not wearing skates.

"What are they doing this time?" Jeff asked.

Squinting, Crista realized they were sitting on folding chairs out in the middle of the ice. She laughed. "I don't know. Let's find out."

Speeding up, they drew closer to the couple. In a minute, Crista realized they were ice fishing. "I wonder if they've caught anything."

"You can fish like that?"

"Sure, they chop a hole in the ice and drop in a line. But it's awfully cold. My dad says it takes a 'hearty soul' to be able to do that."

"And a dedicated fisherman."

"Right."

They cruised closer to the hole and Mr. Wilkins turned around and waved. "Just in time for lunch," he yelled.

Breathing hard, Crista and Jeff stopped by the hole.

"Have you caught anything?" Crista asked immediately.

Mrs. Wilkins knelt down and tugged on a gill line. Pulling it up, two bass, a sunny, and a pickerel flopped out onto the ice. "And we've been at it only a half hour," she said. "The fish are biting for some reason."

Both Mr. and Mrs. Wilkins held lines through the ragged hole.

"How thick is the ice?" Jeff asked.

"About a foot," Mr. Wilkins answered. His jolly face was red and he was thickly wrapped in a heavy hunting jacket, fur hood, and thick gloves. His wife was similarly clothed.

"No skating today?" Crista commented.

"Not much," Mr. Wilkins said.

The dogs finally trotted up behind them and Mr. Wilkins petted Rontu's head.

Jeff suddenly asked, "Can I try it?"

"Sure," Mr. Wilkins answered, handing him the line. "Just don't get pulled in." He turned to Mrs. Wilkins. "I'm going to run over and check the horses."

"Can I come with you?" Crista asked.

"Sure," the big man answered.

As she skated and he walked over the ice, making swishing noises with his thick rubber boots, Crista asked, "Would you teach me to ride, Mr. Wilkins?"

The red-cheeked man glanced at her with surprise. "I thought we already invited you."

"Well, you did. I just wanted to make sure."

"Of course. I'd be happy for the horses to get regular exercise, especially now when they tend to fatten up."

"I'd be willing to clean out their stalls and everything," Crista said. "I think Jeff will help, too."

They reached the beach and Crista watched as Mr. Wilkins checked the horses in the shed. They had thick green horse blankets thrown over their backs. "We'll be going back up soon—about an hour—can't leave them out too long like this," Mr. Wilkins commented. Crista patted Thunder's white path between his eyes.

Mr. Wilkins' gaze moved back out to the fishing hole. There was a sudden shout and Mr. Wilkins made a fist and shook it enthusiastically. "He's got one!"

Crista turned around. Sure enough, Jeff was haul-ing in the line and Mrs. Wilkins was shouting, "Keep it tight! Don't let him run!"

"I've got to see this!" Crista said and hurried back down the beach to the ice. She shot across the ice. Both dogs were barking. Jeff was standing up, pulling hard on the line.

"Don't let it break!" yelled Mrs. Wilkins. "You've got a big one!"

Whatever it was put up a furious fight. Then, with a jerk, Jeff lifted the fish out of the hole. Crista sprinted up just in time to see him grin at the big catfish on the line—about nine inches long. Thick, wirelike tentacles streamed from its lips. It was muddy brown and had a round, ugly head with swiveling eyes.

"A bullhead!" shouted Mr. Wilkins. "We'll keep that one! Or do you want him?"

Jeff continued holding the fish up for all to see.

"Lay him down on the ice and let's get the hook out," Mr. Wilkins said as he shambled up to the group. The catfish twitched and flopped on the ice, making short grunting noises. Holding the tail down with his boot, Mr. Wilkins removed the hook, then pulled up the gill line and threaded it through the fish's gills and out its mouth.

"Catfish are greasy, but tasty," Mr. Wilkins com-mented. "Sure you don't want it?"

Jeff snorted. "If I bring that thing home, they'll make me clean it and eat it all alone. Forget it."

Mrs. Wilkins shook her head. "Some bread crumbs, a little salt and pepper and you've got a real meal. He's at least a quarter pound in the filet." She tugged her line rhythmically back and forth, but nothing struck. Jeff threw his own line back in.

"Mr. Wilkins says we can ride the horses today," Crista said. "I volunteered to clean out the stalls once a week, too. So it looks like we've got a job."

"They could use the regular exercise, and I'll show you how to saddle and groom them," Mr. Wilkins said.

"What do you say, Jeff?" Crista gazed at him, hoping he would agree. But even if he didn't, she knew she would be willing to do it on her own.

To her surprise, Jeff said, "It'll be all right."

"Well, don't be so excited about it!" Mr. Wilkins said, clapping Jeff on the back. "Let's get back in, Carol. I think I've had it for this morning anyway."

Crista and Jeff helped them get their tackle and catch in order, then followed them back to the beach, where they loaded the horses and started up the trail.

"You can come up after lunch. We haven't ridden them much today," Mrs. Wilkins said, turning around in the saddle and looking like Sacajawea or some lady Indian scout hunting deer in winter.

"We'll be up," Crista said.

The Wilkins' clopped up the trail and Jeff and Crista returned to the ice. "That was fun," Crista said.

"Yeah, it was okay."

She laughed. "Is that the way everything is with you? 'It was okay.'" She said it in Jeff's deeper voice, making it sound comical.

Jeff smiled. "It was."

Crista laughed again. "You're weird."

Jeff instantly made a crazy face and pretended to slobber. Crista laughed and they started off down the ice. Suddenly Jeff grabbed Crista's arm. "Look!"

Fifty yards ahead, a buck appeared on the beach. It had a medium rack, five or six points. Crista knew to call it that from Johnny Semms' explanation of how to tell a deer's size. Crista stopped and sank down. "Isn't he beautiful?"

Jeff knelt next to her. "That's the first one I've seen all year."

The two dogs didn't move, but their eyes were fixed on the buck. The deer's big head moved around and gazed at the foursome evenly. It didn't appear afraid or concerned.

Crista slowly took off her backpack, pulled out a notebook and pencil, and took off her gloves. "Just stand still long enough for me to get a few lines down," she whispered.

Jeff watched as she quietly sketched the basic outline of the shore, rocks, and trees. She was fast, getting the shape of the buck's body, head, and rack in just a few fuzzy lines. Everyone seemed to be holding their breath as the buck looked directly at them—an interested but cautious stare.

"I wonder . . ."

"Shhhh," Crista said, "I've almost got it."

She drew the buck's face, looking directly at them. It was a fascinating posture. Crista was managing to catch the feeling of returning the deer's look.

Then, with a sudden spurt and spin, the buck turned, flipped its white and brown tail, and mounted the steep bank between the trees and the beach with a ballet-like leap, then it darted back into the woods .

Everyone breathed at the same time. Crista stopped drawing. The dogs whined. Jeff said, "Well, he's gone."

"He was marvelous," Crista said. "I've never seen one that big before."

"Good thing it's not hunting season," Jeff said. He pretended to aim and shoot.

"You wouldn't really shoot one," Crista asked with an anxious hum.

"No, I'd rather pretend," he said. "But my dad would."

"I'm beginning not to like your Dad so much."

Jeff patted Rontu's head. "Well, maybe my dad wouldn't shoot him. I don't know if he would or he wouldn't." He scrutinized Crista's drawing. "You really are good at that."

"I try," she answered, and flipped the pages back. "Want to see one I did of you?"

"You did one of me?"

She laughed. "Why not? You've got a great smile."

She thumbed through several pages, then found the little portrait she had done a couple days before. Jeff was smiling in the picture as he skated along with his hands behind his back. It was a fair likeness, at least Jeff recognized himself.

He stared at the picture. "No one ever did one like that for me. Can I have it?"

"When it's finished," Crista said. "I've got to do some things with it, first."

"Like what?"

"Finishing touches," she answered, packing up the drawing pad and shoving it into her backpack. She handed Jeff a pack of cupcakes. "Here, for the trip home." She took out a second pack, hefted on the backpack, opened the cupcakes, then pulled on her gloves. They began skating again and eating the sweet chocolate cakes.

"I wish we didn't have to start school tomorrow," Jeff said sadly.

"Oh, you'll like it," Crista answered. "Maybe you'll even be in my class."

"I hope so," Jeff said. He didn't say anything more. They skated in silence till they came around the point.

"Race?" Jeff said first this time, starting to speed up.

"No, I think I'll just enjoy gliding along."

He slowed back down. "Yeah, it's a nice day just for drifting along and falling asleep."

The sound of the blades on the ice was dreamy in Crista's ears. She hoped Jeff really had enjoyed himself. She sensed that he was still struggling with something, though, and she wished he would tell her what it was. It was almost like his mother didn't really want him at all. Crista resolved to say something good about Jeff when she met his father. She just hoped he would come up soon.

·10·

Horseback

That afternoon, Jeff, Crista, and the two dogs plodded up the road to the Wilkins' house. Jeff had come down to Crista's house and, as they walked up the street together, Jeff was throwing snowballs, as usual, at some of the signs different homeowners hung out. One said, "The Platoon Saloon." They were known to be real partiers in the summer. Then there was "In My Sights," and the sign was a picture of a rifle telescope with a deer in its sights. The next house was Mrs. Holmes', a rather crabby old woman who lived there year-round. She had a large sign her husband had put up years ago. It said, "The Holmestead."

Jeff took aim. Just as he threw, Crista spotted Mrs. Holmes in the picture window, watching them. A moment later, she was at the door. "Don't you pelt my sign, boy. Do that again and I'll call the police!"

She stood shaking her fist in the doorway. Crista hung her head and said, "Let's hurry."

But Jeff called back, "It didn't hurt the sign."

Mrs. Holmes ran out into the yard, her head in curlers and her housecoat still on. "What did you say, boy? What did you say?"

"It didn't hurt anything!" Jeff roared.

87

Mrs. Holmes' lips twisted and she shouted, "I'm calling the police!"

She stomped back into the house. Crista was shuddering.

"Jeff, let's go."

"I didn't hurt anything."

Crista pulled at his arm. "She *will* do it, Jeff. She did it to some of the boys last summer and the sheriff came out and everything."

"Old biddy. Someone ought to come out and really break something. Then she'd know what broke really means." Jeff was angry and it was all Crista could do to calm him down and get him past "The Holmestead" and into the woods.

By the time they reached the road to the Wilkins' house, though, Jeff was back to a more friendly mood; Mrs. Holmes was forgotten. They had a good three hours of daylight and Crista was sure one ride on the horses would get their nerves back to a peaceful calm.

Mr. Wilkins was already out in the barn when they arrived. Thunder stood stomping in his stall, blowing air out occasionally with a rubbery snorting sound. Mr. Wilkins suggested Crista try riding Betsarama first.

"She's the gentlest," he explained. "Responds good and doesn't spook easily. Don't have to be worried about her taking off when you least expect it. Not like Thunder." Mr. Wilkins glanced at Jeff. "You going to try it, too?"

Jeff nodded. "I can't let a girl outshow me."

With a teacherly air, Mr. Wilkins showed Crista and Jeff how to place the bit in Betsarama's mouth and draw the bridle over her head, bringing the bottom thong underneath the horse's chin. Then he threw on a blanket and the saddle. "You have to wait till they breathe out," he said with a chuckle. "Horse'll typically hold its breath as you put the saddle on and pull up on the girth—Betsarama's particularly good at it. Got to watch her." He showed them how to hitch the girth in place and tighten it, all the while talking to the pretty horse. "Now, Bets, no foolin' around here. These are good kids and we don't want them falling off and suing us for a million dollars, right? That would put you out of carrots and sugar for days at least."

Both Crista and Jeff chuckled at Mr. Wilkins' easy banter.

"I think you should try Dollar the first time out," Mr. Wilkins commented, as he finished with Betsarama and then led the white horse out of his stall. "He needs some real exercise today anyway. If you want, you can just get used to walking them around the yard. That's simple enough."

Jeff said, "I was hoping to go on Thunder."

Mr. Wilkins laughed. "No, brave as you are, Jeff, I think you'd better start off with Dollar. Thunder just gets too crazy out there in the snow."

Crista saddled Dollar this time, and Jeff put on the bridle. It was hard for Crista to cinch the girth in place. Jeff didn't seem afraid of getting bitten as he tried to push the bit into Dollar's teeth. But when the horse refused the bit, Mr. Wilkins said, "You just stick your thumb under their tongue and they open right up. Most horses would never bite you unless they were just plain mean. And these horses aren't that way at all. We have grandchildren and we wouldn't want them coming out and being around horses that kick and bite."

Finally it was time to climb aboard. Again Mr. Wilkins demonstrated. Taking the reins in his left hand, holding the saddlehorn, he explained that the front rise and saddlehorn were called the pommel. He then placed his left foot in the stirrup. Dollar side-stepped away a bit, but Mr. Wilkins moved with him and, in a moment, plunked down into the creaky western saddle.

"That's all there is to it," he said, climbing back off. "If an old fat guy like me can do it, so can you."

"You're not fat," Crista said quickly.

"Pleasantly plump," Mr. Wilkins answered with a smile. He held Dollar as Jeff followed his directions and placed his left foot in the stirrup. Grabbing the pommel, Jeff hoisted himself up. Dollar sidestepped and swung Jeff out toward the horse's hind leg and flank.

"Whoa, boy!" Mr. Wilkins shushed, but the horse kept moving.

"I'm caught," Jeff yelled, letting go of the pommel. He fell sideways, twisting his foot in the stirrup.

Crista grabbed the stirrup and held on, leaning against the horse's tug. Mr. Wilkins jerked the reins. "Whoa!"

The horse immediately stopped its dancing. Jeff hung from the stirrup, laughing. Then he made his funny, laugh noise. "Nee-hee-hee-hee-hee!"

Mr. Wilkins shook his head and helped Jeff get his foot out.

"Happens to everyone the first time," Mr. Wilkins chided, "but you don't have to act like you enjoyed it. You can't let go no matter what the horse does," Mr. Wilkins ordered. "Now try it again, and this time hang on."

Jeff brushed himself off and stood. "I'm gonna break this horse if it's the last thing I do."

"Don't have to break him," Mr. Wilkins said, grinning at Crista, "just get on him."

Giving Crista one last freaky, clownish look, Jeff tried to remount. This time he made it.

Next, Crista followed Mr. Wilkins' directions and swung herself easily up into the saddle on Betsarama. The leather creaked as she adjusted her backside to the contours of the hard, shiny brown seat. She smiled. "It feels good."

Next to Betsarama and Crista, Dollar stamped and flung his tail back and forth. "I'm ready to go!" Jeff said, rocking in the saddle.

Betsarama wheeled about, and jerked her head up and down, seemingly trying to throw off the bridle and bit. Crista drew back hard and the horse's shoes clicked on the rocky ground inside the barn. Then Betsarama backed up a little, finally standing still and snorting in the cool but not frigid air.

"Put your feet in the stirrups and this show is on the road," Mr. Wilkins said, patting Dollar's neck. "He won't do anything you don't tell him to do, so just be calm and hold on tight to the pommel with your left hand, if you want, while you direct with the right."

Mr. Wilkins explained about turning the horses right and left by using the reins, how to stop by pulling up, and how to get the horse moving by a slight heel jab in the ribs.

Crista gave Betsarama a gentle kick and immediately the beautiful brown horse sparked forward into a trot and clopped out the front door of the barn.

"Keep your head down," Mr. Wilkins called as she exited the barn, bending low so the top of the doorway didn't catch her in the forehead. She heard Jeff clopping behind her, and then Mr. Wilkins shriek, "Head down."

She heard a thud and turned around in time to see Jeff lean back in the saddle and grab his head. "Ouch!"

"Just nicked you! Don't worry about it!" Mr. Wilkins called as he ran along behind them. He raised his eyebrows and shrugged at Crista, as if to say, "You win some, you lose some."

Both horses trotted out into the sunshine and Mr. Wilkins opened the gate to a small, snow-filled pasture. A muddy track where the snow had been trod down wound all the way around in an oval inside the fence. "Walk them around a bit and keep out of the deeper snow!" Mr. Wilkins noted. He climbed the fence and sat facing the inside, watching.

Crista and Betsarama trotted on the path with Rontu and Tigger at their heels, both dogs prancing along as if they also wanted riders, saddles, bits, and bridles themselves. "You wouldn't like it!" Crista cried to Rontu as the albino dog moved past them and marched regally out in front of the procession.

"How do you feel?" Crista called behind her as she listened for any signs of distress from Jeff.

The bigger boy was lounging in the saddle, looking like he was in complete control. "Great!" he said with confidence. "I'm ready to gallop."

Smiling, Crista gave Betsarama a little kick and the horse speeded up into a faster trot. "Now for the real stuff," she mumbled to herself. The horse wheeled around the ring, catching Tigger and Rontu by surprise, forcing both dogs to bound forward to get out of the way.

Dollar immediately began trotting behind Betsarama. Crista looked back and saw Jeff bouncing in the saddle, the horse's trot making him look like he would catapult off the white back any moment.

"How do you like it now?" Crista called.

Jeff's teeth chattered as he talked. "I like it! I like it!"

Crista came around the far end of the pasture and bounced along toward Mr. Wilkins. He watched them with twinkling eyes, his body hunched over, holding a little red datebook in his hand.

"You're doing great!" he called.

"It's fun!" Crista answered.

For the moment, Jeff seemed to be perched on the roof of a highrise in the middle of an earthquake. He was having trouble staying upright, trouble guiding the horse, trouble keeping his feet in the stirrups. Dollar jerked left and right in response to Jeff's ragged touch on the reins.

"You have to keep those reins straight," Mr. Wilkins yelled, as Jeff and Dollar pranced, trotted, and shambled around the corner.

Jeff was all but thrown out of the saddle. "I don't kn-kn-know how to-to-to kee-keep my behind fi-fixed in pla-pla-place," Jeff stammered as he went by.

Crista guided Betsarama back onto the straightaway. "How fast can she go?" she shouted to Mr. Wilkins.

"Better slow her down now," Mr. Wilkins answered, "or she'll be galloping. She likes to move."

Deciding against a faster ride, Crista pulled up on the reins and Betsarama immediately jolted to a walk. The two dogs had stopped to sniff one of the posts along the track on the far side.

Dollar, however, didn't slow down. Jeff was still bouncing along in a trot, when the white horse overtook Betsarama and Crista and splashed mud and snow against Crista's legs.

"Hey!" Crista yelled.

Either Jeff was out of control or else he wanted the horse to go. Either way, Dollar was working into a pacing gait. Jeff shouted, "I forget how to stop!" He seemed totally confused and kicked Dollar in the side again. Instantly, Dollar leaped out of the trot into a full canter.

"Yo!" Mr. Wilkins called, jumping off the fence and onto the track.

Jouncing back and forth in the saddle, Jeff didn't seem to have any idea what to do. Dollar went straight for the curve, then cantered around. Crista was sure that Jeff, leaning way out, would hurtle off. But the boy held on.

A moment later Jeff pitched and rolled backward, almost falling off the horse.

Crista nudged Betsarama. "Let's go."

The horse didn't need a second order. What seemed like an instant later, the cold air was blowing in her face as she hurtled down the track, tugged along by the powerful muscular feel of the horse underneath her. It was the motion and sensation of raw power. She wanted to cry, "Wheeeee!" except for the fact that Mr. Wilkins had raced out onto the track yelling, "Slow down! Slow down!"

But now Jeff seemed to be having fun. "It's great! This is great!" Dollar loped around the end curve and back onto Mr. Wilkins' side of the straightaway.

Crista and Betsarama were right behind him, Crista leaning forward and holding onto the saddlehorn with all her strength. "Just don't fall," she murmured, "just don't fall," as the wind blew in her ears and the air seemed to envelop her face in an icy battering of tiny stilettoes.

Both horses came around to the straightaway. Mr. Wilkins took a position in front of them, waving his arms. "Slow down! Stop!"

Moments later both horses came to an abrupt stop. Holding onto the horn, Crista flattened out backward on top of the horse and kept her balance.

However, she looked up just in time to see Jeff roll over Dollar's neck and topple down in a clump into the mud and snow in front of Mr. Wilkins. Jeff didn't move.

Mr. Wilkins shouted, then ran forward. Dollar reared and turned. Crista jumped off Betsarama. "Oh no!" she cried. "He can't be hurt!"

Jeff moaned as he rolled over, face up on the track. Mud and ice clung to his face. His cheeks were scratched and his upper lip was broken and bleeding.

Bending over him, Mr. Wilkins lifted Jeff's head up. "Anything broken?"

Crista hurried up and knelt down in the snow. Rontu and Tigger were there, too, both tails wagging, their eyes staring in wonder at this boy who seemed to get everything wrong.

"I don't think so," Jeff wheezed and sat up.

Searching his face, Mr. Wilkins said, "Are you sure you can stand?"

Crista's heart seemed to crack right through her breastbone. This time he would be really upset. But suddenly Jeff smiled. "I did it. I rode the horse, didn't I? I even galloped."

Mr. Wilkins laughed. "Not very well. But you were on top for most of the ride."

Chuckling, Jeff hauled himself to his feet. "It was great. It was really great. I don't even ache or anything."

"You will tomorrow," Mr. Wilkins said, patting the boy on the shoulder. "Let's get you cleaned up. Go on into the house. Meanwhile, Crista and I will get these renegades back into their stalls."

A half hour later, Jeff was patched up and Mr. Wilkins gave the children and dogs a ride back down to their homes. "I guarantee you won't fall off like that again," Mr. Wilkins promised as they rounded the curve.

Immediately, everyone gasped. A police car stood outside Jeff's grandparents' house.

· 11 ·

Dump Dogs

"Oh, no," Crista cried, "the sheriff is here!"

Expelling a long sigh of anger and fear, Jeff said, "I guess we don't need to ask what that's about."

Five minutes later, Sheriff Thomas gave Jeff a stirring lecture about patriotism, the American Way, and how to steer clear of old crab-apples like Mrs. Holmes.

"She's always calling us about something," the sheriff said, "and she pays her taxes so we have to respond. But if you're going to throw snowballs, son, there are plenty of trees to aim at."

"I understand, sir," Jeff answered.

"Good!" The sheriff smiled and left. Crista was still shaking when the police car finally disappeared up the road. She said goodnight to Jeff and decided to go right home—and not even look in Mrs. Holmes' direction.

That night Jeff called to tell Crista that his grandparents were upset, but they weren't blaming him, so it hadn't turned out too badly. Crista felt she could relax after hearing that.

"Want to visit my friends Johnny and Nadine today, when we ride the horses?" Crista asked as she stood in Jeff's doorway on Saturday morning. They had both been riding the Wilkins' horses every afternoon since the first day of school. Jeff was good with Dollar, and kept insisting he was ready for Thunder, but Mr. Wilkins wanted to see more improvement on the milder horse first.

"Let's," Jeff said, pulling on his coat and stepping out into the morning sunlight. The snow had melted a bit and the air was warmer the second week of January than it had been in a month. Crista had begun to feel very comfortable with her new friend.

Rontu and Tigger tagged along as they walked up the road that led to the highway and the Wilkins' farm road. They talked about school, Mrs. Bevans, and a science project that was coming up on electricity. Crista volunteered to do a project with him.

"You would, really?" Jeff answered.

"Why not? Mr. Camping encourages kids to work together whenever they can."

"But what could we do?"

"Let's ask Mr. Wilkins when we get there. I bet he'll have something right from the start."

Jeff kicked at clumps of snow and Crista searched the woods for something new to draw as they walked. She didn't think of Jeff as a "boyfriend," just as a friend. She had never had a male friend like this before, and it gave her a rich, tingly, joyful feeling every time she told someone that she and Jeff were "just friends."

They came to the main crossing and the mucky entrance to the farm. Both kids ran across, laughing as the dogs barked and yelped behind them. "You're getting to be pretty good at riding, you know," Crista said as they started up the drive.

Making his funny howling laugh, Jeff said, "Next week I'm on Thunder for sure."

Jeff was his old self again, winging snowballs and talking about sports and racing and being a private investigator when he grew up. Ahead, the sunlight glinted off the aluminum roof of the barn. A weather vane on the front cupola squeaked in the slight wind as it changed direction.

"I think I'd like to do a picture of you on Dollar this time," Crista said as they stepped into the driveway.

"I thought you wanted to visit Johnny and Nadine today?"

"I mean when we take a break. You'll have to pose, though."

Jeff cocked his head in a dramatic pose. Crista laughed.

"I'm doing it for my art teacher. Mrs. Rutter wants me to do something with 'movement,' so I wanted to capture you cantering along or something." Crista was still taking the art lessons that she won at Thanksgiving. She had also won a trip to Philadelphia's renowned Museum of Art and $200. The three paintings that had won the contest still hung in the local library.

"Just so I get to gallop," Jeff said. "Galloping is great."

"I like it too," Crista answered. "But cantering is like being in a rocking chair."

"Yeah, that's exactly it!" Jeff said suddenly. "I was trying to think of what it was like last night."

"We'll just have to be careful if we go to Johnny and Nadine's," Crista mused as they stepped into the barn.

"How come?" Jeff said, then called, "Mr. Wilkins, we're here."

No one answered, but Crista heard several horses snort in their stalls. She hit the light switch and looked down the line of stalls. "They're all here. Guess Mr. Wilkins is in the house."

They turned off the light, and went up to the farm-house and knocked on the door.

"How come we have to be careful?" Jeff asked again as they stood on the porch.

"Bears around the dump, and dump dogs, and rats." Crista explained about the town dump that was on the road back to the Semms' cabin.

"You ever seen a bear?" Jeff suddenly asked. "That would be incredible."

"No, but Johnny has. It's mainly the dump dogs, though."

Mrs. Wilkins opened the door. "Well, snow or shine, here they are!" She called back into the house, "Rollie, the kids are here."

As Jeff and Crista stepped into the warm, yellow wallpapered kitchen, Mr. Wilkins came through the dining room doorway with a newspaper in his hand. "Gonna ride like the wind today, huh?"

Crista smiled. Jeff whooped like an Indian, then grinned with embarrassment.

"We were thinking about taking a ride over to Nadine and Johnny Semms' house," Crista said. "They live over on the next mountain, down the road to the dump."

"Well, our road connects with that road down aways. It'll be a long ride, but if your rear ends are up to it, it's all right by me." Mr. Wilkins glanced at his wife, Carol, and she nodded.

"Go ahead," she said. "The horses haven't been out for a long ride for two days now."

Out in the barn, Jeff looked at Thunder and petted his nose. "In a week, it's just you and me, Thunny, my boy. Then we'll see what you're made of." But Jeff saddled Dollar as always, while Crista took Betsarama. The air was not as cold that morning, though it was definitely below freezing. It would feel good to get out in the air and clop along without having to think about school, parents, or anything else.

When they both trotted out onto the road, with Rontu and Tigger sniffing out rabbit holes through the dense trees on either side, Crista enjoyed the bite of the wind and the crisp wintry air. "I love it when it's like this," she said, not even thinking that Jeff might be listening.

Jeff responded, "When are you going to draw me riding?"

Adjusting the little blue backpack, Crista replied, "I'll use the dump as a backdrop."

Jeff wrinkled his nostrils. "I've never really been to the dump."

"Oh, it's a wonderful place," Crista said, half joking. She did enjoy an occasional sift through the junk, looking for something usable. Once she had found a whole box of costume jewelry. She had cut up the jewelry to try her hand at making homemade necklaces, earrings, and brooches. Another time, she discovered a like-new bassinet that she gave to Nadine before the twins were born. "Johnny shoots rats down there sometimes," she continued as the horses trotted down the road toward the valley between the mountains. "He's a good shot, too."

"With what kind of gun?" Jeff asked.

"Twenty-two, I think. He let me shoot it a couple times. It was kind of fun. But I didn't aim at any rats. Just some cans."

"How long have you known Johnny and Nadine?"

"About five months. Since September."

"You found the dogs in the woods, too, didn't you?"

Crista had told Jeff a little about how she had met Rontu one day while hiking through the woods. She had befriended him with goodies, cupcakes, and hot dogs and began leaving a pile of treats every day by a special tree she had discovered that had lovers' initials carved into it. She called it The Love Tree. As she and Rontu came to trust one another, she decided to talk her father into letting her keep the Great Dane. Her father was against it, but then a series of harrowing events happened: Tigger got caught in a trap and Rontu was shot in the leg by a hunter. Dr. Mayfield decided the dogs were hardy, good friends, and worth having around.

"They were dump dogs, all right," Crista answered. "But even a dump dog can be lovable at times." She whistled affectionately at the two dogs as they roved around in the woods by the road. Rontu stopped and twitched his ears, but Tigger seemed excited by some scent and didn't notice.

The road wound through the trees and the children fell silent as the majesty of the mountains, the sky, the woods, and the scents and sounds of the forest mixed around them. It was a beauty Crista longed to capture in her art, but which, at this point, she felt quite incapable of doing. She hoped one day to be a real artist, making a living by her paintings and drawings. She knew it would be hard, but that was what life was all about, or so she figured.

She had never discussed her belief in Christ with Jeff. She thought about it occasionally. But in fact, she didn't even know if Jeff had any background in religion. Her father told her frequently to respect other people's faiths, even if you were convinced they were wrong. The only way to win a person to Christ was through compassion, kindness, giving, and plain love. And, of course, telling them how He had affected your own life.

Thinking about these things as they clopped mile after mile down the blacktopped road, Crista watched blue jays, chickadees, sparrows, and crows flutter about in the air and woods around them. Now and then a squirrel or chipmunk spoke in a squeaky chirp that Crista always enjoyed. She remembered a poem by Robert Frost that she had memorized in fourth grade:

> The woods are lovely, dark, and deep,
> but I have promises to keep,
> and miles to go before I sleep,
> and miles to go before I sleep.

She smiled as she remembered how nervous she had been when reciting it in front of the class that first time, then later at a special presentation to parents and teachers.

"What's your favorite thing to do?" Crista suddenly asked, as her reverie faded.

"Squashing bugs," Jeff answered immediately.

"Yuck!"

"Just kidding." He laughed and in the silence of the woods he whooped for the first time that afternoon.

"You should have been an Indian," Crista said.

"I am, part," Jeff said suddenly. Then, after a silence, he said, "No, I'm not. I just made that up."

Crista looked over at him. *With a gray or blue Civil War cap, he'd look just like some young captain at Gettysburg.*

"Well, what's your favorite thing to eat?" Crista asked again. The way the horse's hooves clopped the ground in the silent woods echoed eerily. She loved the silence in a snow-filled forest. For her it was such peace.

Jeff's voice broke her out of her reverie. "Ice cream, I guess."

"Oh. What kind?"

"Chocolate chocolate chip. With really big chips in it—whole chunks of chocolate."

"Yeah, I like that too. Maybe I'll get some next time I go to the store. We can have you and your grandparents over some night for dinner."

"Does your Dad usually make dinner?"

"Oh, we switch off." Crista wiped her forehead. For all the cold, she was sweating as she rode the hot horse. Even below 32 degrees you could still get hot enough to sweat if you exerted yourself. "I try the new things. He does the standards."

"Standards?"

"Hot dogs, hamburgers, frozen vegetables. The really easy stuff."

"And what do you make?"

"My mom had a lot of recipe books, some really old, and it's fun to look through them and create something we've never had before."

"You never talk about your mom much." Jeff was parallel to Crista. Each horse had slowed to a walk. They stepped down the road, guiding the horses now almost without thinking.

Crista sighed. "Sometimes it's hard. She was a great person to me. She taught me everything about cooking and sewing and drawing. She was an artist too. In college she did a lot of artwork. We still have some of her paintings. But after I was born, she said I was 'her art.' I always kind of liked it. She called me 'H.A.' for 'her art' a lot, especially when she was really happy. I miss her a lot...but I'll see her again in heaven."

"You believe in God, huh?" Jeff asked, looking across at her. Both horses had come to a stop in front of the turnoff to the dump road and Johnny and Nadine's.

"I do—a lot," Crista said, feeling a quiet flush prickle onto her face.

"How come?" He gazed at her with those firm, green eyes that gave no indication of anything but absolute sincerity.

"Well, all my family does and my mom did especially. And my dad, too. But I guess the main reason is because I accepted Jesus about a year ago and ever since then He's been so real to me. In a way, knowing Him doesn't change everything or suddenly make everything better. But it does make me feel happy and like I don't have to be afraid of things I used to be afraid of."

"Like what?"

"Mainly dying. Dying suddenly. When my mom was killed, I got this fear that the same thing was going to happen to me, every time I walked on the street or when I was in the car. It was really scary. Then, when I met Jesus, that fear just went away because I knew if I died, I'd be with Him. And with my mom, too."

"You really believe that, huh?"

"Yeah, I do." The horses snorted and stamped at the bend and Crista waited till she couldn't endure another moment of silence. "What do you believe?"

"I..."

"I know—you don't know."

Jeff chuckled. "Guess I say that a lot."

"It's okay. Have you ever learned anything about Jesus?"

"Not really. When I was smaller, we went to church now and then. But it was so boring, I never paid any attention. I just drew on whatever papers I could find."

Crista laughed. "That's how I started with art. I used to draw in church, too. It does get boring. But Sunday school is okay. I like it, actually. We play games and do crafts and things and our teacher tells some pretty good stories. He really plays it up. He's in college."

Turning Betsarama onto the road toward the dump and the Semms' cabin, Crista said, "If you want, we could take you when we go tomorrow . . . or some other Sunday."

Jeff looked at her with sudden interest. "You would?"

"Sure. That's what Christians are supposed to do anyway—invite everyone to find out who Jesus is and what He did. So I'd be really happy to have you come."

Jeff laughed. "When I was little, we used to have these people come to the door and leave all kinds of pamphlets and booklets and stuff. My dad always got real mad about it."

The moment he said it, Crista glanced at Jeff. His face had his somber, dark look again. "Yeah, he'll probably be coming soon," he said, almost to himself.

"I thought he was supposed to come last weekend," Crista said, suddenly remembering.

"He couldn't," Jeff answered quickly, turning Dollar onto the dump road.

"Will he take you home?"

"Yeah, probably," Jeff answered. His voice now had that distant sound, like he was not really paying attention.

Crista asked again, "Are you sure your father is coming up here, Jeff? I mean..." She kicked Betsarama to catch up to him.

Jeff jerked the reins and stopped abruptly. "Of course he's coming. Why wouldn't he?"

A fierce light shone in his green eyes and Crista almost decided not to ask any more questions. But gritting her teeth she pushed ahead. "Jeff, are you sure he's going to come? I mean you're always saying he is, but then..."

Jeff looked away, his jaw flexing and unflexing. "He's coming. He just had a lot of things to do."

"Well, are your parents divorced?"

Jeff blinked and gradually the horses just stopped in the middle of the road as if resting. Jeff stared straight ahead.

"You can tell me, it's okay," Crista explained, her heart suddenly beating hard. She didn't know what else to say. "You don't have to hide it. You should really accept it, I guess, and..."

Jeff turned and stared at her angrily. "My father will be coming soon, all right? That's all you have to know." He kicked Dollar, and the white horse sprang forward. He kicked again and, in a moment, the horse was thundering down the road in a full canter.

Crista nudged Betsarama. "Let's go, girl." She looked up at Jeff. "Now what's wrong with him?" she muttered, then shouted, "Jeff! Please! Stop!"

Betsarama moved easily into a canter. Suddenly, Crista was really scared. *What if Jeff's father wasn't coming back? What if he was never coming?*

Betsarama was beginning to breathe harder so Crista slowed her down to a trot. They were moving up to the dump anyway, and she thought they had better not make too much noise when they went by. But Jeff had already turned the bend and disappeared.

"What is he doing?" Crista muttered between clenched teeth as Betsarama cranked it up close to a gallop, but not quite.

· 12 ·

A Visit

Crista passed the parking lot to the dump, and spotted some dogs nosing around in the debris. The dump was a large landfill stuck back in the woods away from the lake and houses. Beyond the parking lot was a drop-off into a natural valley that had been dug out years before. The area around the lake was not heavily populated, even in the summer, so the dump never seemed to be close to filling up.

Black, acrid smoke drifted skyward. Crista spotted the attendant's battered green pickup truck at the far side of the parking lot. Betsarama passed by on the road without even a look in the dump's direction. Immediately past the dump, the road veered off to the right. The rough-paved road ended. The road back to the Semms' was just a rutted dirt road in the summer, but now the snow was tamped down by tire tracks. Johnny had been in and out so many times in the last weeks with the birth of the twins, that he didn't need to plow it. His truck plowed through the snow easily anyway, with its big radial tires and "lifters" that kept the whole machine high above the axles. Except for the night of the twins' birth, when he had gotten stuck in a snowbank, he had never had any trouble.

As Crista came around the curve, she saw that Jeff had slowed to a walk. He was hunched over in the saddle. Crista reined Betsarama in and brought her back to a trot, then a walk as she came up next to Jeff.

"What's wrong?" she asked.

"Nothing."

"Don't start that again."

"Nothing. All right?" He glanced at her with fierce eyes, then turned back to the road.

Crista decided not to push it. "It's just about another mile in," she said, telling herself it was just another mood. The horses clicked up to a brisk trot.

She felt like her jaw would bounce off any moment. Trotting was definitely the most difficult gait she had experienced so far. But she had never really galloped yet, unless what just happened was it—and she was sure it wasn't. Cantering was easy, though, like sitting in a rocking chair that was propelled by a rocket! And walking was, well, walking. Nothing to that. Just the swaying back and forth of the horse's rump as you plodded along. Cantering so far was her favorite.

"Nadine's the woman that came with you the night we had the fire on the beach, right?" Jeff asked. His voice had that tired sound, like he was too tuckered out to fight whatever he was fighting.

"Right. She's really pretty. And she just had twins. They've been living up here since last summer. And Johnny's a lot of fun but, of course, he works during the day most of the time. He works at a gas station on the road into Hawley."

"Which one?"

"Exxon, I think. I forget."

"Yeah, that's at the corner."

They both slowed down to a walk. The dogs had stuck behind at the dump, and Crista suddenly stopped Betsarama and turned around in the saddle. "Rontu! Tigger! Get out of that garbage!" She couldn't see them, though.

"Should we go back?"

"No," Crista answered, "they'll be along. Just visiting old friends, probably." She wrinkled her nose in disgust. "I can't imagine what it must be like for a dog to have to scrounge around in a dump for every scrap he gets."

"Lucky for them they found you."

"Yeah, but it's a mutual benefit."

"Oh, yeah? How?" Jeff tried to smile as they walked along, but she could tell he was thinking about something else.

"They eat the stuff I don't want and I get someone to walk me to the bus stop each morning."

"That's not too bad."

They came around a bend and a moment later the Semms' cabin broke into view. Smoke rose from the chimney. A chilly wind riffled through the trees and shook snow down from the boughs. One shirt hung on the clothesline, looking stiff as concrete. They came around the back of the cabin where the outhouse sat and another storage barn where, once, Rontu and Tigger had slept before Crista's dad had decided to let her keep them. Rontu and Tigger raced around the bend and caught up to them with happy woofing and more snuffling.

"Maybe Nadine will have some cookies or something just baked!" Crista said excitedly. "And wait till she sees the horses. And you'll get to see my first painting of Nadine. Come on!"

Crista didn't even try to keep the joy out of her voice. She hadn't seen Nadine in over a week now, and she longed to hold the twins and hear her friend's melodic, husky voice.

"Hi!" Nadine called, as she opened the front door and looked out at Crista and Jeff tying the horses to the post at the edge of the porch. "I didn't expect you today. And with a friend!"

"Just wanted to make sure you're still feeding those babies!" Crista said excitedly and rushed to Nadine. Both friends crushed each other in their arms. Jeff stood back, shifting his weight nervously. Nadine hugged him next, though Jeff kept his arms at his sides. "Come in, come in," she said, her voice trembling with joy.

"They're happy as dump dogs in fresh garbage," Nadine said, as she held the door open for Rontu and Tigger. "Guess they should come in, too. They'll be wanting to make sure the babies are surviving my mothering!"

Rontu nuzzled Nadine's hand and Tigger gave her a friendly lick, then both dogs promptly dropped down in front of the crackling fire.

Crista bent over the crib in the main room and looked down into the two tiny, dark, pinkish faces. "They're so beautiful, don't you think, Jeff?"

For the first time Jeff smiled. "What do I know about babies?"

Nadine brought out the hot chocolate and, as she and Crista talked, Jeff walked around the cabin, stared at the trophies of deer, moose, bobcat, and squirrel and then picked up Johnny's hunting rifle, hung on deer feet bent to hold it over the fireplace. He sighted along it, then put it back.

"Johnny will show you how to shoot it," Nadine said.

"I'd like that," Jeff replied.

After a half hour of talk, Crista decided it was time to take the horses back. "We can't let them get too cold."

Mounting up, Crista and Jeff said goodbye.

"We'll be back soon!" Crista called as they walked out of the yard.

"Feel better?" Crista asked as they stepped out into the ruts of the dirt road beyond the clearing.

"I'm okay."

"Johnny really will let you shoot the gun."

"That would be fun."

The dogs ran out ahead of them, sniffing and looking every which way for signs of rabbits, foxes, or squirrels.

Suddenly Crista heard a great commotion—dogs were howling behind them! She twisted around in time to see a pack of about a dozen dogs leap out of the woods and come careening up the road toward them. She was about to yell, but Betsarama didn't wait for a kick. Crista was almost jerked out of the saddle as the horse sprang into a gallop. Dollar had spooked too, and Jeff was holding onto the pommel.

"Grab the horn!" he yelled. "These two are going!"

Crista flailed away, trying to find the pommel. The dogs howled behind them, several as close as 10 feet now.

The horses were in a full gallop. Crista bent down, her whole body feeling like it would catapult off into oblivion at any moment. Jeff's face was white. Both horse's were side by side. Rontu and Tigger had gotten behind them and were just in front of the pack.

Crista tried to pull up on the reins, but Betsarama didn't respond. Crista was sure the dogs wouldn't attack the horses. But now she had lost her stirrups— her feet dangled and she was bouncing all over the saddle, holding onto the pommel with her left hand and the reins with her right.

"Hold on!" Jeff yelled.

"I can't!" Crista cried. She was sure that at any second she would fall off. But she pressed in with her thighs and tried to get her legs hooked back into the stirrups. Jeff was holding up well. He didn't appear afraid and he was leaning forward, barely holding the pommel—like a real cowboy.

Both horses threw up clumps of dirt and snow. The dogs yowled and barked behind them. Tigger and Rontu were in the back, fighting off a band of four dogs while the rest of the pack pursued Crista and Jeff.

"They've got Rontu!" Crista yelled.

"I can't stop!" Jeff answered.

They came around the bend. The dump was just ahead.

Both horses were clearly out of control now. It was all Crista could do to hang on. She leaned forward, trying to get better balance, like a jockey.

Then she spotted Mr. Clemmons, the dump man. He ran out into the road with a shotgun.

"Don't!" Crista called as both horses went by.

Mr. Clemmons yelled, "I'm not going to shoot them."

Just as they passed, the gun roared. Both horses cranked up their velocity until the wind whistled in her ears. Crista couldn't look back but, in a moment, she realized the dogs had stopped. Mr. Clemmons' gunshot had scared them off.

Moments later they came to the turnoff. Both horses slowed only enough to make the curve without slipping. They still thundered down the road. Betsarama's neck and flanks were wet with sweat and froth dripped from her mouth. *This was one scared horse,* Crista thought, and then she realized she wasn't afraid anymore. She was simply enjoying the ride—they were both galloping.

Gradually, though, as the silence of the forest engulfed them, the horses calmed down and slowed to a walk. Then they both stopped in the middle of the road. Jeff panted, "I thought I was going to die."

"Me too," Crista said. "But it was great!"

"Yeah."

"Where are the dogs?" Jeff twisted around to look back. Rontu and Tigger appeared moments later.

"Guess they fought everyone off."

"Would they really have attacked us?" Jeff asked.

"I don't know, but the horses weren't about to find out."

As the dogs caught up and the horses stopped breathing so hard, Crista jumped off. "We'd better walk them for awhile."

"Yeah," Jeff said. He dismounted, too.

They ambled along the bumpy pavement in silence for another 15 minutes, both of them too tired to speak. Finally, they came to the Wilkins' farm. They both headed straight for the barn.

Inside, Mr. Wilkins greeted them. "Looks like you really ran them," he said immediately, his eyebrows knitted with worry.

"It's not like we wanted to," Crista said quickly.

"We had a run-in with the dump dogs," Jeff added.

"Yeah, they can really give the horses a scare." Mr. Wilkins led them to the stalls, then helped take off the bridles and saddles. With a slap on the rear, he sent each horse into the warm stalls.

"You have got to tell me about this one," Mr. Wilkins declared.

"One thing is for sure," Jeff answered.

"What's that?" Crista asked.

"I'm ready for Thunder now."

Mr. Wilkins grinned. "That you are, boy. That you are."

Crista gazed at her friend with admiration. Jeff had to be one of the bravest kids she had ever met. He really wasn't afraid of anything—once he tried it. But there was something else about him she liked, a magnetism, an effortless sense of fun that he often exhibited when he wasn't in one of his moods.

She wondered again why he had those moods. They seemed to come upon him and wreck whatever he was doing for the time being. But when he snapped out of it, he really was a lot of fun. He was good at so many things. And even his hope of seeing his father—even if that was an impossible dream—he would find a way through it. That she was confident of.

She only hoped he didn't go crazy like he had in Philadelphia, breaking all those windows. *What would make a person do that?* she wondered. She couldn't imagine it. But whatever it was, she was going to stick by him. They were friends and that's what counted. Friends should be loyal to one another, even if they do make mistakes now and then.

·13·

Suspicion

The school placed Jeff in Crista's class as they had hoped and Crista discovered another thing about Jeff: He was smart. Math was especially easy for him, but he also had a flair for making up stories and writing them out.

Early in the first week of school, Crista and Jeff had to decide on a science project and also a creative writing story. Jeff came up with the idea of showing how a nuclear bomb worked—even though they both learned that that was secret information. It was surprising how much you could find out from books. He and Crista worked on a model that they fashioned out of papier-maché. It turned out to be a rather gooey project and not as flashy as they had hoped. But they still had several months to do it, so there was no big rush to get it done.

Crista, for the creative writing, had the idea of doing a cartoon strip like they have in newspapers. Jeff had to come up with the lines and she had to do the drawings. They decided on something called "Kitt and Fitt," a cat and dog—a little like Garfield and his sidekick, Odie. It continued to be a fun experience and drew them closer together.

For a whole first week, Crista and Jeff rode the horses or skated after school, then went home for dinner. In the evening, Jeff came over to Crista's house and they worked on their projects. Then Jeff would go home and she would see him next at the bus stop up at the corner. Jeff was always cranky in the morning, and frequently he slept on the bus during the half-hour ride to school. Crista thought they might be staying up too late on their various projects, but really, Jeff was home by nine o'clock. Nadine suggested that maybe he was a night owl rather than a morning glory, two expressions she used for people who were energetic at night or in the morning, but rarely both.

Then on the Friday evening of the second week, Crista and her father were alone—Dr. Mayfield was reading the paper and Crista was working on a painting of Thunder. Jeff had not come over because he had gone out to eat with his grandparents at an expensive restaurant. Crista's father suddenly said in the middle of his reading, "Looks like they've got a fix on who's doing these break-ins."

"Who?" Crista asked, looking up. Her father had grown a mustache over the last few weeks and he looked very dashing to Crista—like Kevin Costner in *Dances with Wolves*, one of her favorite movies.

"They're sure it's kids, now."

Crista stared at her father, her heart suddenly speeding up with fear. "How come?"

"They've taken to shooting up the house with BBs, probably from a pellet gun or maybe something else."

Swallowing hard, trying to keep the fright off her face, Crista barely breathed. "Where did they last break in?"

"Still down the cove. They have a watch on it now, police cars drive through every hour. But they haven't caught them. Police think they're doing it after midnight."

Immediately Crista thought of all the things she knew about Jeff: smart, wily, daring, and owns a slingshot. In addition, he had broken the windows in his school, and he was very angry inside about things. Above all, he was always tired in the morning. And—this was the biggest one—everything had started shortly after he had come to live with his grandparents.

These thoughts were so frightening that Crista looked down and noticed that her hand was shaking as she gripped an extra-fine paintbrush.

"Keep your eyes open, Crissie," Dr. Mayfield said. "If you see anything unusual, let me know, Honey, okay?"

"I will," Crista said a little too quickly. She knew she had to talk to Jeff about it, the sooner the better.

She had the chance the next morning just before lunch. It was Saturday and they had decided to skate out to the island, have a picnic, then walk up to the Wilkins' house and ride the horses all the way out to the highway. After stepping onto the ice and skating with lazy, free strides, Crista decided to bring up the issue.

"Jeff, have you heard anything about the break-ins that have been happening down the cove?"

His eyes fixed ahead, not paying close attention, Jeff answered, "Just what my grandfather told me from what was in the paper."

"You don't think anyone from our school could be doing it, do you? The police think it's kids, you know."

"Yeah, but from the school? Naw." Jeff glanced at her uneasily. Crista wondered if that was a sign.

"The last thing I heard was that the people who did it, did it with a slingshot."

Jeff suddenly laughed. "I know. Kind of made me think they'll try to blame it on me."

"Oh, they'd never do that."

Turning to her, Jeff said with some bitterness, "If you're a bad egg, or if you've ever done anything wrong, you're always the first one they come after."

"Why do you say that?"

"Because that's what they have been doing with me—at least my mother—about other things."

Taking a gulp of air, Crista said, "Jeff, you wouldn't do anything like this, would you?"

There was a sudden silence. Jeff stared ahead and Crista could see his jaw flex and unflex with anger.

"So you're on their side too, huh?" He didn't look at her. His eyes were hard, set.

"No. But you do have a slingshot, and you did... well, you know."

He started to speed up and then he spun around and stopped in a cascade of ice flakes from the skate blades. "I suppose you think I'm doing it. I suppose you think I'd really do something like that. Yeah, you're all alike. There's no one I can trust."

"Jeff, please," Crista stopped, facing him. "I just..."

"Yeah, you just this, you just that. You're like all of them. I thought you were different. But you're not. I'm going home." He dug in and started forward.

"Jeff, please!" She hurried after him. "Jeff!"

The boy bent into his strokes and shot out way ahead of her. There was no catching up. He went straight for his dock and the shore. She caught up to him as he threw off his skates on the beach.

"Jeff, I don't think you did it! I never did!"

He stared at her. "Then why did you ask the question?"

She looked away, terrified. "Because...because..."

"Because you suspected me—like everyone else. Like my mother, like my grandparents, like everybody. Just because I did one thing wrong. I thought you were different, but you're no different."

Crista blurted, "Jeff, I asked you because I wanted to be sure, so if there comes a time when I have to choose sides, I can choose yours."

He stared at her, his lower lip stuck out. He started to turn. He stood in the snow in his thick thermal socks. For a long moment, they faced one another angrily. Then Crista said, "Jeff, you're my best friend and I want to be completely on your side. And if I wasn't sure you didn't do it, I couldn't feel that way. But I want to believe you." She gazed steadfastly into his hard eyes, refusing to blink or show the slightest sign of weakness.

"Why?" he said fiercely, spitting it out like a firebrand.

"Because...because you're like my brother. You're my best friend. I don't know. I care. I really care, okay?"

He shifted his weight uneasily, then took a deep breath, looked up and smiled hesitantly. "I knew you wouldn't dump me."

Crista suddenly grinned, waves of relief washing over her. "Friends never dump each other."

"I'm sorry. I guess it just hit me wrong."

"It's okay."

He sighed and started to sit down. "Still want to go to the island?"

"Of course. Race?"

"Yeah."

"I'm taking a head start!" Crista turned and was off. She knew she would need every extra second to beat him.

By the time she reached the first point, Jeff was on the ice and after her. She was already tired and panting, but she pushed on around the points. He caught up to her in the straightaway to the island. But as he started to pass her, he suddenly slowed down and stayed right with her.

"You're not racing," Crista wheezed.

"I'd rather skate together today."

She smiled at him. Things were okay, she thought. He really wasn't involved. Whatever happened now, she knew she could defend him.

·14·
Ideas

"I can do it," Jeff told Mr. Wilkins. "I think I can handle him. We've been riding almost every day now for weeks. I really think I can do it."

Raising his eyebrows and shaking his head, Mr. Wilkins glanced at his wife and then at Crista. She and Jeff had walked up to the farm shortly before lunch and found the Wilkins' out in the barn, singing and brushing down the horses.

"Why not, Rollie?" Mrs. Wilkins suddenly said. "Thunder isn't that crazy. He obeys you."

"Yeah, but I weigh over 250 pounds," Mr. Wilkins said with another shake of his head.

"I weigh one-o-two," Jeff quickly added. "And I'm not afraid."

After another skeptical look that finally settled on Jeff's determined green eyes, Mr. Wilkins said, "All right. Crista on Betsarama, me on Dollar, Carol on Lukas, and you on Thunder—and we stick together. Nothing faster than a trot until I say so."

"All right!" Jeff shouted, thrusting his hand into the air like the classic football-goal dance of a triumphant running back.

Thunder was wonderfully tame that afternoon. Jeff rode him like an equestrian master. The foursome went as far as Nadine and Johnny's house, where the Wilkins' cooed over and cuddled the baby twins and then proudly pronounced them the "two most beautiful babies in Northern Pennsylvania."

On the way back, no dump dogs appeared and everything went uneventfully with Jeff even firing up Thunder to a full gallop at one point. At the end of the ride, he said that he and Thunder were now best of friends and he would never ride any of the other horses without first telling Thunder why he had to do such a thing. Mr. and Mrs. Wilkins laughed heartily at Jeff's enthusiasm.

On the walk back home at two-thirty, Crista decided to bring up the Winter Carnival, now less than two weeks away—the first of February. "I have this costume," Crista explained, "like a horse. Last year I was the tail and my friend Jeannie was the head. We did some funny things and it was a real hit."

"Are you doing it with her again?" Jeff asked.

"She moved to Ohio last summer."

"Oh." He obviously wasn't catching on.

"I was hoping to find someone else who would do it with me, or maybe even something else, something new."

Jeff kicked at frozen clumps of snow and ice. "Who would you do it with?"

Letting out an exasperated sigh, Crista finally blurted, "You, for heaven's sake."

"Me?"

"Who did you think?"

"I never..."

"It doesn't matter. If you don't want to do it..."

Suddenly Crista felt hurt. Sometimes Jeff could be so dense.

"No, I do!" Jeff immediately answered. "I thought it was something you only did with another girl or something."

"Good grief," Crista exclaimed, "do you think girls never do anything with boys?"

Giving her a sly look, Jeff grinned. "I never had anyone who really wanted to do things with me like you, that's all."

It struck Crista with a hot flush. *He really didn't have any close friends.* It was amazing to her. *How could anyone grow up and not have a few friends, one or two at least?* As she thought about it, though, she realized Jeff hadn't paired off with any of the boys in sixth grade either. He only hung around with Crista. For all his bluff and bluster, he was a very shy person.

"What would you like to do?"

Wrinkling his brow with thought, he said after a silence, "Something we both could do, huh?"

"Right."

"You don't want to do your horse thing again?"

"Well, I did it last year and you're really not supposed to repeat, though I guess it wouldn't really be a repeat since I'm doing it with a different person."

"No, we have to think of something cool, really cool."

Crista gazed ahead at the road through the woods. She looked at the snow-covered pines, heavy with the white frosting. A special, almost eternal silence hung over the woods that made her feel like sinking down into her jacket and turtleneck sweater and cuddling in the warmth, peering out through the top as if through a submarine periscope.

Breaking the silence, Jeff asked, "Does it have to be comical?"

Crista shook her head. "No, there's pairs dancing, and all the freestyle skating things like in the Olympics. It's just that the comedy was a little easier for me. I really tense up when I'm alone in front of a group."

"Yeah, me too."

"Okay, so then it has to be something that we could kind of hide behind."

"A costume."

"Yeah."

"But I'd like to do something comic," Jeff said, shaking his head. "That would probably be more fun."

"I'd feel more comfortable with it, I think," Crista answered.

They walked on, their feet making shushing noises in the snow and their pant legs rubbing on each side with a swish.

"I've got it!" Jeff suddenly exclaimed. "Shoes."

"Shoes?"

"Yeah, we could dress up like two old shoes, you know, like the ones you see in the 'Old Lady Who Lived in a Shoe.'" Jeff spoke excitedly, his eyes shining. "We could, like, do a sort of dance and even have the emcee—your father or Johnny or maybe Nadine—announce what we're doing. Like we could do a pigeon trying to ice skate. And pigeons are pigeon-toed, so we would keep crashing into each other."

Crista guffawed with interest. "And then we could show a duck skating—duck-toed and we'd fly apart, then bash down on our rears as the duck's feet come out from under him."

"Great!" Jeff exclaimed. "We can think of about five things."

"I could make the costumes, too, with Nadine's help. They would be like cowboy boots or old-time shoes with huge laces up the front."

"Great!" Jeff said again. He was grinning widely. "It'll be hilarious!"

Noticing that they had sped up in their excitement, Crista slowed down. She became more serious. "It'll be hard to pull off, Jeff, if we don't really work at it."

"But we will. Every day."

"What about the horses?"

"We'll do that, too."

"There isn't that much time." Crista gave him a searching look.

"We won't go to school for the next three weeks."

"I wish!" Crista said with a laugh.

"Oh, we'll figure it out," Jeff said confidently. "It's just great to do something with someone, that's all."

"Yeah, I'm excited," Crista said. They both stepped out of the woods onto Rock Road for the jaunt down to Jeff's house. As they neared the corner, Jeff suddenly said, "Uh-oh."

"What?" Crista asked.

"My mom—look."

Instantly, Crista spotted the strange car in the driveway, a gray, expensive-looking one.

"That's her," Jeff said, his enthusiasm obviously deflating.

"You'll be all right," Crista said quickly.

"Yeah, but I never know what she'll pull next."

"Want me to come in with you?"

Shaking his head, Jeff said, "No, I'll have to deal with it. The worst she can do is decide to take me home or something, and I don't think she'll do that."

•   •   •

"What happened?" Crista breathed into the phone, keeping her voice low so her father couldn't hear.

"Nothing really." Jeff's voice was matter-of-fact, almost shapeless, almost bored. But underneath it, Crista detected anger and bitterness.

"She didn't say anything?"

"'Hi, Jeffie.' That was about it."

"She didn't hug you?"

"No, we never hug or kiss."

"Good grief," Crista answered. "You must be pretty mad."

"Not really."

"Jeff, come on. I'd be angry."

"I'm not. Really. But I did find out something else."

"What?"

"I think my dad's trying to do something, maybe get custody of me or something. I heard them talking about it when they didn't know I was there, really hush-hush. And then, when I made a noise, they stopped and my grandfather said, 'Let's discuss this later.' So I think something's up."

"Do you want to live with your dad?"

"I wouldn't mind it."

The phone was suddenly muffled, and Crista heard him talking to someone, then his voice came back on.

"Sorry, my grandma wanted to know if I wanted some pie."

"Is your dad ever coming up, Jeff, really?"

The phone was covered again and there was a silence. Then Jeff came back on. "Maybe I'll write him and tell him about the carnival. Maybe he would come up to see it."

"Where does he live?"

"In Phillie."

"You know the address?"

"Of course." Something in Crista doubted everything Jeff was saying, but she had nothing to go on other than the fact that Jeff always talked about his father in low, secretive tones, like he didn't want anyone else to hear. She decided not to ask anymore about it.

"Did Nadine and you do any work on the costume yet?" Jeff asked.

"We just decided this afternoon," Crista answered. "I'm not that quick."

"Well, I'll help you. I really want to do this."

"Okay, tomorrow after school we start. I think some kind of wire frame will work, maybe made out of papier-maché or something like that."

"I'll do whatever you say."

Crista smiled. "All right, I'm giving the orders. Be here tomorrow after school, three o'clock sharp."

"Aye aye, sir." He laughed and said, "Goodnight," then hung up.

Crista leaned back in the chair by the phone table in the hall and sighed. Sometimes Jeff seemed so complicated. *Did he really have a father who was interested in him at all? Was he involved in any of the break-ins?*

The first question was difficult for her to answer. Time would tell on that one. But the second one—she still wasn't sure. She only wished the police would catch someone and that that someone not be Jeff.

·15·

Dancing Shoes

The next week, Crista and Jeff fabricated the "shoes" in her basement, with occasional help from Johnny and Nadine, and some constructive comments from Dr. Mayfield. Crista and Jeff stood inside the ankle part of each shoe, while the toe and boot stuck out about three feet in front. They were high, painted brown, and had huge black laces Crista had fashioned from some black material she had in the loft.

Jeff had the idea of putting a hinge inside the toe so it could be moved up and down and sideways for various motions and positions. It would be quite a daring spectacle. Saturday came with a full day for working on their routine.

After some discussion, Dr. Mayfield was passed over in favor of Johnny Semms for announcer. Johnny was to give a verbal picture of what the shoes were "doing" on the ice. The laughter was supposed to ignite as the shoes "did" whatever it was Johnny proclaimed.

Both the "pigeon-toed" and "duck-toed" ideas were easy to work out and choreograph, as Nadine kept calling it. Jeff and Crista hopped forward in the pigeon routine, finally colliding and falling over one another.

131

Johnny, practicing his banter, intoned, "So much for pigeon-skating, folks."

The duck skit involved both skaters starting off and veering out until they both came down—bump—on their behinds with the toes up in the air. Johnny commented, "Ducks were never meant for the ice. That's why they go south in the winter!"

Nadine had come up with the idea of "Old Mother Hubbard at her first dance." Crista wiggled her toe, then tapped it impatiently in the manner of a girl waiting for her first dance. Immediately, Johnny shifted to "Little Boy Blue" trying to decide whether or not he would ask the "Old Mother" to dance. Jeff hunched his shoe up over Crista's in a scared-stiff, shy-as-all-get-out boy trying to work up his courage to ask the girl.

They still needed two more skits for a full three-minute show. Suggestions were fired back and forth, but Johnny finally hit on one. "How about Old Mother Hubbard doing 'the Stomp'?"

"The Stomp?" Crista and Jeff exclaimed. "What's that?"

"A dance." Johnny told them about a dance called "The Bristol Stomp" that his mother used to tell him about. He showed them how to do it and said he could even get a copy of the record.

All they needed now was one more skit and they would be finished. Meanwhile they practiced the four they had and both Nadine and Dr. Mayfield laughed heartily as Johnny shouted out his part from the top of Crista's dock. Jeff and Crista caught on quickly.

Strangely enough, Dr. Mayfield had an idea for the last bit. "Hopscotch," he said. "It's perfect. You can do just a little hopscotch and maybe some jumping rope too."

It worked. Again, Crista figured out the way to do the stunts in the hot shoe costumes and she and Jeff continued to hone their routine during the next week. They went horseback riding only three times, but Mr. Wilkins wasn't unhappy about it. He said, "Horses aren't everything. And anyway, I don't want Thunder to forget I'm the real master and not Jeff."

Then the week before the carnival, Mrs. Holmes, the lady who had been angry at Jeff for throwing snowballs at her sign, stopped by Crista's house one evening. Dr. Mayfield answered the door, but when Crista saw who it was, she went to the door and listened.

"Dr. Mayfield," Mrs. Holmes said, "I'm going out of town for two weeks. You wouldn't mind keeping an eye on my place, would you?"

"Of course not," Dr. Mayfield said. "Crista walks by it on the way to the bus stop. She can report in daily."

"Well, if it wasn't for that boy down there at the end . . ." Mrs. Holmes said, giving Crista a hard look. "I know you and he are friends, but I think he can be destructive. I don't want to come home to a shambles, like what has been happening down the cove."

"We'll keep an eye out," Dr. Mayfield assured her.

When he closed the door, Crista seethed, "Jeff would never do anything to her house, Daddy. But it would serve her right the way she acts about him."

"Calm down, Honey," Dr. Mayfield said, putting his hands on her shoulders. "Mrs. Holmes is just an old lady, not very strong anymore, and a widow. She doesn't really have anything against Jeff."

"She did call the police that one time."

"And the policeman was very nice about it, right?"

"Yes, but Jeff shouldn't have had to be questioned. It was a stupid snowball on her stupid sign."

Chiding her, Dr. Mayfield said, "Just keep out of trouble and all will be fine."

"Keep Mrs. Holmes out of trouble, I'd say."

Dr. Mayfield grinned and sat down with his paper. "Anyway, you've got the carnival to keep you two busy. And those horses."

·16·

Being Bad

"It makes me nervous when you bring that sling-shot," Crista said the moment Jeff stepped out into the cold.

"Aw, I just wanted to show you something."

"What?"

"How good I'm getting."

They walked up Rock Road toward the main highway and the dirt road through the trees they often used to go to the Wilkins' farm.

"Watch this," Jeff said, aiming the slingshot at a fencepost.

The slingshot snapped with a little shush and a copper-colored BB ricocheted off the post into the snow. "See," Jeff said. "I'm getting as good as a sharp-shooter or a commando or something."

"I don't like it. You know..."

"Yes, I know all about the people who are sup-posedly breaking into houses and all that. I'm not it, okay?"

"It just gives me a shiver every time I see you with it, that's all."

"You still don't trust me." Jeff was taking aim at a chipmunk sitting on a branch chewing some of the birds' food.

"*Jeff!*" Crista grabbed his hand and pushed it down. Jeff gave her a look of defiance.

"I'm not going to hit your precious wood creatures, okay? Good grief!"

"Jeff, I don't like it. What were you aiming at?"

"The chipmunk. But I wasn't going to shoot. Anyway, a little BB wouldn't kill one, so don't worry about it."

"No, it would just maim him for life, that's all."

Jeff aimed at another tree. Sure enough, the BB hit in the center of the trunk and bounced off into the snow. "It's a good idea though."

"What's a good idea?"

"Shooting out windows."

"*Jeff!*"

"Quit saying Jeff! It's making me nervous."

"You should be. That slingshot is dangerous and people will suspect you, don't you realize that?"

"But I haven't done anything." Aiming the slingshot around at various things, he centered on something by a house, a piece of wood on top of a small shed. "Watch this."

He fired. There was a thunk, then a sudden tink.

"It hit the house, Jeff!"

The boy's face went white. "We'd better look." They stepped through the foot-deep snow and spotted a nick in the paint just underneath a window.

"That does it," Crista exclaimed. "I'm not going anywhere if you have that slingshot. And you'll have to tell the Sutherlands, who live in that house, what you did and offer to fix it."

"But it isn't anything, and no one would ever even notice it."

"Promise me you won't shoot it within 100 feet of any house ever again."

He grinned. "I promise." He gazed up at the window. "Boy, I could have hit it and broken it. That would really be trouble."

"To the hilt," Crista answered. "Let's go."

Jeff stared up at the house. "I wonder what is in these places."

Crista gazed at him in blank horror. "What are you suggesting?"

"I don't know." He punched her shoulder. "Just razzin' you, that's all. I would never really break into one. It does sound kind of adventurous, though."

"It sounds like big trouble to me." Crista looked into Jeff's eyes, trying to see if there was anything beyond what he was saying. But he had his usual playful, just-scarin'-you look she was quite used to by now. He cocked the slingshot, then groaned.

"Well, I'm out of BBs, so there's nothing more to worry about." He showed her where he kept the BBs in a pouch on his belt.

"I don't know what the fascination is that boys have with slingshots," Crista said, shaking her head. "It's really dumb."

"It makes us feel powerful," Jeff said, grinning. "Like we can deal with anything that comes along and protect the womenfolk."

"Yeah, right." Against her better instincts, Crista laughed.

They trudged back out to the road and went up through the woods toward the farm. They were ready for the Winter Carnival, so Crista was glad to be taking a break and getting back into horseback riding. She had missed the last three days because she was putting the finishing touches on their shoe outfits. And she had gotten way behind on her drawing. Her teacher would be upset! But she had finished one good picture of Thunder the previous week and that had been good. Mrs. Rutter was not too demanding, even though she had been pushing Crista to try more in-depth pictures of country scenes.

The ride at the Wilkins' was wonderful. Mr. Wilkins commented on Jeff's slingshot, saying, "You'd better not shoot it while Thunder is underneath you. You may end up in the lake."

The next day Jeff and Crista practiced again for the Winter Carnival. It was coming up that weekend. With Nadine's coaching and Johnny's clear announcing, they had the routine down. Surely it would be the hit of the year!

Still, Crista worried about the signals Jeff seemed to be giving off. *Was he or wasn't he involved in the cove break-ins? If he wasn't, why did so many things make it look like he was? But on the other hand, when would he have time for such things? It had to take a lot of time, and he would have to sneak out of his grandparents' house late at night. Wouldn't they have caught on to something by now?*

Then there was the problem of Jeff's father. Crista still wasn't convinced the man was ever going to show up. Jeff hadn't talked much about him lately, but something sounded very fishy. *And if Jeff was making it all up, that made it even worse. Did he have serious mental problems on top of everything else?*

Crista wasn't sure whom to go to and again she decided to talk to Nadine about it. The night before the carnival, Nadine and Johnny had come over to see Dr. Mayfield about some things concerning the twins. It ended up that they stayed for dinner and, as always,

Crista and Nadine did the dishes together. It was the perfect time to talk.

After some small talk about the babies and the weather and Johnny's new job at the hospital that Dr. Mayfield had gotten him, Crista finally said, "Nadine, have you ever thought someone might be doing something very bad but you couldn't be sure and worried about it all the time, wondering if he might or might not be capable of it, and it just ate away at you inside until you thought you might explode?"

Nadine smiled at Crista. " That was one long question there, little sister."

"Okay, let me make it smaller. It's about Jeff."

"I figured that."

Crista took a deep breath. "I'm beginning to think he really is doing some of those break-ins. Some of the things he does . . . I don't know what to think."

"Like what?"

Crista told her about the slingshot a few days before, and also the run-in with Mrs. Holmes and some of the things Jeff had said afterward.

"Well, how would he be doing it?"

"That's what I can't figure out. It seems impossible."

"Wouldn't there be tracks?"

"Tracks?"

"From Jeff's house. Through the woods to one of the broken-into houses. He can't drive there, so he'd have to walk."

"There are millions of trails all over the place."

Shaking her head, Nadine said, "Not that many. And there aren't that many people around the lake here in the winter. Surely you could find one. You know what Jeff's boot tracks look like, don't you?"

"I could find out. I'd probably remember."

"Or you could just follow him, watch the house some night."

"But that would be like spying." Crista sighed. This was getting far more complicated than she had thought it could be.

"Still, if he's doing it, I think he'd leave a trail somewhere. The best way to do it might be to go to one of the houses and see where the trail leads."

"But wouldn't the police be doing that?"

Nadine squinched up her face and nodded. "Yeah, I guess. It was just a thought. But I think you ought to give your friend a break, Crissie, don't you?"

Nodding, Crista agreed. "I shouldn't be so suspicious, I guess. It really gets him mad."

"It would make me mad if Johnny were always accusing me of something I didn't do and wouldn't do in a million years. But that's the way it is sometimes. You just have to take things as they come."

"I guess I should pray about it, too."

"Now there's a good idea." Nadine smiled, then reached out with wet, soap-sudded hands and hugged Crista. "It'll be okay. I just don't think a 12-year-old kid could be doing all that stuff."

That night, before bed, Crista prayed long and hard. Regardless of what Jeff might be doing or thinking, she knew God loved him and would work at doing the things that would turn Jeff's life around.

After praying she looked at her alarm clock. Her father usually arose around seven-thirty on Saturday. If she got up at five and went down into the woods with a flashlight to look, she could be back well before seven. It would be creepy, but it could settle everything once and for all.

·17·

A Spy

The alarm beep-beeped at five-thirty. Crista jumped out of bed and listened. There was no stirring from her father's room; the snoring droned on as usual. She smiled. "Not even an earthquake could get him up at this hour," she mused as she cautiously turned on her light.

Then she sighed unhappily. *"Do you really want to do this, Crista?"* she asked herself. *"Do you want to find out Jeff's behind these break-ins?"*

She closed her eyes and prayed. *"Please, Lord, let this turn out for good."*

Then she shucked her pajama tops and bottoms, dressed, and stood at the door. Her father was still snoring. She turned out the light, then quietly shut the door behind her. She tiptoed down to the cellar stair-well door, listened again, then creaked it open.

The flashlight was just where she had left it the night before. She flicked it on and off quickly. Finally, she started down the stairs.

Suddenly, the thought flashed through her mind. *What if it's not Jeff, and what if you run into them?*

She froze. "Them" was the real burglars. She could be done for. In the light she blinked, then she crept

downstairs and stood at the workbench. She quickly
wrote a note.

> Dear Daddy,   I went down the cove this
> morning. I had to find out if Jeff was doing
> the break-ins. If I'm not back by seven you
> know something went wrong.
>   Love, Crista
>
> P.S. Please find this note if I don't come
> back!

She chuckled at her joke, but it was more a prayer.
She stopped and thought about what she was doing,
then prayed again. *"Lord, don't let anything go wrong.
Please!"*

She opened the door and stepped out into the
barely gray morning. The sun wouldn't rise for over
another hour and it was very dark out, although the
back spotlight was on, so the woods were partially
illuminated. She hurried down the trail to the lake.
Johnny had kept it shoveled for the Mayfields as
thanks for all Dr. Mayfield's help with the twins and
Nadine, so it was smooth going. When she reached the
beach, the stars were still out as was a bright moon. She
flashed the light over the beach and noticed a number
of tracks. Hurriedly, she bent over, looking at several
different ones to see if she recognized Jeff's bootprint.

He wore hunter's boots, usually, when he went
through the woods. They were rubber, with a tread on
the bottom like raised squares. It was distinctive and
she was sure she would recognize one—if it was fresh.

There were none that were new, so she headed down
the beach to Jeff's house, keeping to the shadows. It

was scary in the dark and if the moon hadn't been shining off the ice and several of the lake lamps across the way still burning, it would have been as dark as the plague of Egypt—the "darkness that could be felt." Fortunately, it was not *that* dark.

She cruised along, shining the light close to the snow looking for fresh tracks. But everything was a day or two old. She could tell by the overlapping tracks and the way the snow had blown over many of them.

When she reached the Halperns' house, she looked at the dark cabin. Jeff's room was black. She thought about tapping on his window, but then he would want to know why she was out that early. What would she say? "Just looking at the moon." He could be so suspicious! She was already coming close to betraying him as it was. She didn't want him knowing she had been out there.

She walked up the path to the house, still keeping among the trees. When she reached the house, she thought of how he might do it. She wasn't sure, so she circled the house looking for tracks... anything....

Eventually she came to Jeff's corner room. The hill was steep in the back, but the side window wasn't that far off the ground. Edging along the siding, she worked her way up to the window. It was still a bit above her head, but after taking off a glove, she reached up to feel the window.

Warm air! The window was cracked open.

With terror seizing her heart, she looked down at the ground and turned on the flashlight.

Fresh tracks! Right under the window.

"No!" Crista whispered, barely able to breathe. "*No!*"

Again she reached up to the window. Yes, warm air. Crista blinked with fear. It couldn't be! No, it couldn't!

She peered again at the tracks and knelt beside them. They led up to the road. She thought she could never follow them on the road, but when she got there, his track in the two-day-old snow was visible. He had gone down the road toward the main part of the cove. Precisely where the burglaries had been. Crista's heart was pounding so hard, she thought the whole neighborhood must hear. But she knew she had to see this through.

She followed the tracks, keeping out of the street-light areas as best she could. They led in a straight line past her house, past the last few houses on her street and then down a cul-de-sac to the next street. Then suddenly they turned down a driveway.

Still following, Crista's fear mounted. *What if Jeff was part of a gang? But how could that be? He'd only been there for a month!*

Then what if he was doing it alone? And what if she caught him in the act? What might he do to her? He was just crazy enough at times to really hurt her. But surely he wouldn't hurt her!

"But what if?" she murmured. Again she tried to still the hammering in her rib cage.

"Okay, I'll just see if I can see him, that's all," she said to herself. "I won't say anything to anyone. I'll talk to him first."

But what about the flashlight? Could she risk turning it on?

She had to. She couldn't see the tracks otherwise. *Then why don't you come back when it's light?*

"It may be too late then," she said in a murmur.

No, she had to go on. This was the best chance she had to know the truth. And if it wasn't proved after this, then it would never be proved because he would never be friends with her again.

She followed the tracks down the driveway. At the bottom of the closed-up house, they veered off to the left. She began following the tracks carefully through the woods. At times he had obviously stopped and knelt to look around. She paused at those places, then pressed on. Soon she came out back at the lake. The tracks, though, were still clear. Winding around beached docks and huge rocks along the shore, she went slowly, carefully, stopping now and then to listen. The wind had been picking up and the first signs of gray appeared on the horizon.

Then the tracks suddenly went back up into the woods. This was getting so nerve-wracking, Crista thought she might explode. For the hundredth time she switched on the light and followed the tracks through the woods for another 30 feet. It was so creepy, she knew she had to be crazy to do this, but now it was a matter of life and death!

She saw that the tracks came to a large pine tree— and stopped.

Just stopped!

She stared at them.

"Where?"

He came right out of the tree at her. Whoever it was landed right on her, threw her down, and covered her mouth before she could scream. His grip was viselike. She couldn't move. She fought to get up, to throw him off, but he had her. Her heart was so loud she couldn't hear. Her head seemed about to explode.

Then Jeff's voice resounded low and cool in the quiet: "Crista!"

She stopped struggling.

"Crista! Don't scream. It's me, Jeff."

She lay still.

"I'll take my hand away if you won't scream."

She nodded assent.

The moment he removed his hand, she whispered, "Jeff, what is this?"

She could see him grinning in the light. He picked up her flashlight and flicked it off. "Looks like we had the same idea," he said.

"What?"

"You're out looking for them, right?"

Crista's breathing slowed and her heartbeat came back, closer to normal.

As she blinked and said nothing, his face suddenly changed. "You're not out here looking for them, you were tracking me!"

"Jeff!"

"You were, weren't you? You still think I'm the one doing it!"

"Jeff, no, it's not..."

"Oh, I get it now. You went to my house or something this morning and you've been following me, right to here. Is that it?"

She sagged and nodded wearily. "I'm sorry. I had..."

He clapped his hands on his sides. "Well, that does it. I'm leaving. I thought I might see them here, but it turns out I'm the one who was seen."

"Jeff, I'm sorry."

He got up and dusted himself off. The slingshot hung from his belt. "Yeah, well, guess that makes two of us. Some friend you are."

"Jeff, please, I'm really ... I'm really confused. Honest! I just didn't know what to think. It's all jumbled up in ..."

He began stalking away, down to the lake. She jumped up and ran after him.

"Yeah, and you'll probably think that I was just down here looking for a house to break into," he said. "So it really doesn't matter what I say or do. You'll never believe me. Never. Just like everyone else. And here you said I was your best friend. I'd hate to be second best if this is the way you treat them."

She grabbed his arm. "Jeff, it's not like that. But we've only known each other a short time. Please understand, I was only doing it ..."

"Yeah, for my own good. Just like my mom and my dad and my grandfather and everyone else. Everyone's doing everything for my own good. Then how come I never see the good of it, huh? Tell me that." He turned and faced her. "Do you have an answer for that one?"

Crista stared at him. It was past six-thirty and the sun had begun to rise. Golden light fired across the eastern sky over the lake. Birds chittered here and there. Things were coming back to life.

Crista couldn't think of anything to say or do. She hung her head. "I'm sorry. Will you forgive me? Please? Just this once? Just forgive me and I swear I'll never do it again. Please?"

She raised her eyes until she was looking into his. He flinched away, then came slowly back to her and sighed. "We still have to do the Winter Carnival this afternoon, right?"

She nodded. There were tears in her eyes and she was sure he was going to say no to everything, including that.

But suddenly he sighed. "I guess I have to give it more time. All right. I forgive you." His voice softened. "I guess I haven't exactly proved to be the best friend either, scaring you with my slingshot like that yesterday. So I guess we're even."

"I don't want to be even, Jeff. I want to be best friends still."

He smiled. "All right. It was an honest mistake. And who knows, maybe I really was scoping out the house to burgle it."

"Don't say that!"

"All right. Let's get home and get some sleep."

·18·
Truth

The Winter Carnival started at one o'clock in the afternoon. Crista and Jeff came on shortly after two and were a hit. People laughed as Johnny spoke over the microphone and the "two shoes" did the motions. It worked so well that they won both the "Most Creative Act" and "Funniest Act" prizes. Both awards came with $25 gift certificates from Smalley's, a local clothes store. All the way home, Crista, Jeff, Nadine, Johnny, and Dr. Mayfield talked about their success. When they let Jeff off at his house, though, Crista got out and said she would walk home.

Dr. Mayfield roared up the road and Crista turned quickly to Jeff. "Thanks," she said.

"For what?" Jeff answered. "You did everything."

"It wouldn't have worked without you, and it wouldn't have been as much fun."

"Yeah," Jeff said, "it was fun. And don't worry about this morning. I guess a lot of things just looked like it was me. But it's not. I hope you believe that."

"I do, Jeff."

He smiled. "You're the best friend I ever had, Crista."

Hugging her chest in the cold, Crista continued, "I hope you weren't disappointed."

"About what?"

"Your dad. Your mom. Not even your grandparents went."

He looked away and sighed. "My grandparents had a funeral to go to. They wanted to come, but it didn't work out. My mom, well, my mom is my mom. I guess I just have to accept the way things are." He stamped his feet and blew vapor into the air. He looked a little uncomfortable, but Crista said nothing.

"And my dad. Yeah, my dad." Jeff looked down at his feet. "I don't think my dad will be showing up this year." For a moment he hesitated, then he raised his eyes to look into Crista's.

"I guess you might as well know, so you don't think I'm completely crazy. My dad's been gone for over three years. I keep hoping...I even wrote him a few letters. But they all came back—'address unknown.' My mom was mad about it, but I keep hoping." He shrugged and Crista could see the wetness in the corner of his eyes.

"I'm really sorry, Jeff."

He shrugged again and sighed. "It's all right. I'm used to it. You have to accept it, I guess."

"Accept what?"

"That no one, well...that no one really wants you around."

"I want you around."

There was a sudden silence, then Jeff sniffled. "I really hate this."

Instantly, Crista put her arms around him and hugged him tight. Then he was crying and heaving and shaking and she didn't know what to do. But as quickly as it came, it was gone.

Wiping his eyes, Jeff said, "I'm sorry, I'm really sorry, Crista. You must think I'm a complete baby."

Quietly Crista said, "I don't think that."

"Yeah," he said, nodding and sighing heavily. "It's okay. Sometimes I think I can stand it, and then sometimes I just want to run. I want to tear up to the farm and saddle up Thunder and ride, just ride. I don't even know where I'd go. Just away ... like they do in movies ... into the sunset ... disappear. Sometimes ..." Still wiping at his eyes, he turned to her, "Sometimes I wish I'd just suddenly disappear and it would all be over."

"I don't want you to disappear."

"I know."

"Then don't. Please!"

He nodded and gave her a sad smile. "I promise I'll let you know, okay?"

She held out her hand. "Punch it!"

He punched it.

"Okay. I'll see you tomorrow."

"For sure."

• • •

The next week, the second week of February, was a major thaw although the lake was still frozen solid. Toward the end of the week, Dr. Mayfield went down to look, and he and Crista listened to the news for any reports of weak spots in the ice. By Friday, there were a few parts that glistened from surface melting, so Jeff and Crista stayed close to shore when they skated.

They rode Thunder and Betsarama every other day at least and helped Mr. Wilkins muck out the stalls and put in feed and hay. Jeff seemed much happier than he had been, now that there was no pressure for his father to "show up." He told Crista it was a relief that she knew. He told her he didn't like keeping it from her, especially now that she was convinced he wasn't involved in any of the burglaries. Several times they talked about trying to catch the criminals who were committing the break-ins, but they both decided the police had better handle it.

Saturday morning Crista and Jeff were about to head off to the Wilkins' house when Jeff saw the sheriff's car pull up his driveway. He and Crista were standing at Jeff's dock down at the lake.

The moment Jeff saw the sheriff get out, he ducked and hid under the dock. "I know something's happened, I know it."

Crista tried to calm him. "Don't jump to conclusions."

He pulled Crista down underneath. "Look, if he's looking for me, I have to know. Okay? I'm not going through this anymore."

"But what could be wrong, Jeff?"

"I don't know. But why is the sheriff pulling up to my grandparents' house?"

"We should find out."

"You find out. I'm staying here."

"Jeff, you're innocent. There's nothing to be afraid of."

"Yeah, that's what they told me before."

"Before?"

"After I broke the school windows. Then every prank that happened, the police were at my mom's door."

Standing and leaning over the edge of the dock, Crista peered up at the house. "All right," she said, "let me find out. Don't do anything crazy, all right?"

"All right. I won't move. No one knows I'm here yet."

"Okay. Just be calm."

"All right!"

Crista sped up to the beach, dodging boulders and docks and everything else pulled up onto the beach for winter. In a few minutes she stepped through the back door of her house. "Daddy?"

"Crista!" Her father was standing looking out the front window, but when he heard Crista he spun around. "The sheriff was just here."

"What for?"

"Mrs. Holmes' house was vandalized. They're looking for Jeff."

Freezing, Crista felt her skin tighten and her heart pound. Then she said with fervor, "Daddy, Jeff didn't do it."

"Honey, we'll let the police handle this. I think the best thing to do..."

She shrieked, "The best thing is for everyone to leave Jeff alone!" Her voice cracked and she turned and ran out the back door.

"Crista! Crista, come back!"

She was halfway down the path before she realized she might be leading everyone to Jeff's hiding place. But she had to let him know. She didn't know what they could do, but Mrs. Holmes was probably bent on blaming it on him. She stopped at her dock and peered around its edge trying to see if her father would follow.

When no one pursued her, she breathed easier. She knew the whole thing was a mistake and Jeff was innocent. *But who knew what the sheriff would do? Would he throw Jeff in jail? Could they even do that? If only the person who had been doing the break-ins didn't have a slingshot!*

She sprinted down the last 20 yards to the dock. Still staying low, she sprang behind the dock, ducked down and looked in. "Jeff! Jeff! It's okay. We just have to . . ."

Looking underneath, though, all was quiet. He was gone.

·19·

Running

"He got caught," Crista shrieked, half in her mind, half out loud. "No, no, he can't have been!"

She rushed up the trail to the Halperns' house. The sheriff's car was still out front. Racing around the corner, Crista paused by a window and looked in. The sheriff was standing at the door, and Mr. and Mrs. Halpern were talking to him. Was Jeff in his room?

Hurrying around to the front, she paused at the door, now closed. Blinking back the terror, she tried to think of what could have happened. *Had they come down to the lake while she was gone? Had Jeff surrendered?*

Seconds after the thoughts registered, she knew there was nothing else to do but knock and find out what was going on. Hesitantly, she opened the front storm door, then grasped the knocker. She clicked it three times.

Immediately the door flew open. It was Mr. Halpern.

"Crista, we're so glad to see you!" he said. "We were so worried. Do you know where Jeff is?"

Standing in the doorway, Crista couldn't move. "He's not here?"

"No, we haven't seen him for over an hour. The sheriff..." Mr. Halpern motioned to the man standing behind him in a tan and dark brown uniform. He was tall, with a brown mustache and bright blue eyes. He even looked friendly and not upset at all. "The sheriff wanted to ask some questions. Mrs. Holmes' house was vandalized. But we're very sure Jeff didn't..."

"Oh, I know," Crista said immediately. "Jeff has not done any of that stuff. I know he hasn't."

"Well, where is he then?" Mrs. Halpern said, stepping forward. The sheriff moved out of her way as she walked toward the door.

Shaking her head, Crista said, "I don't know. He was down at the lake. I went home. And I thought he would come up here."

The sheriff stepped forward. In a deep, mellow voice he said, "Look, when you find him tell him not to worry about a thing. We're quite certain it doesn't involve him. But it seems Mrs. Holmes, well, I guess you know she's a bit eccentric."

"Yes, he had that run-in with her a few weeks ago," Jeff's grandfather said. "He's had a very bad time of it this past year and he's been so excitable lately. And then with all this crime..."

"We're going to find them, sir," the sheriff said, stepping out. "When he comes home, just give me a call." He handed Mr. Halpern a card. "And assure him there's nothing to worry about. He's not a bad kid and no one's out to get him."

Mrs. Halpern's eyes teared up and Mr. Halpern put his arm around her.

"The boy has been very upset about his father," Mr. Halpern explained. "He and my daughter divorced three years ago and his father hasn't visited once or even called. It's a tough thing for a kid."

"I know," the sheriff said. "Anyway, hang in there. Maybe he saw my car and just got scared and is hiding somewhere. He's probably watching us from under a porch right now." The sheriff laughed. "I'll be waiting for your call. And don't worry about Mrs. Holmes. We've done plenty of business with her, I can tell you that."

Mr. Halpern chuckled, but Mrs. Halpern was still upset and Crista stood on the porch trying to think of what might have happened.

After the sheriff got into his car and roared away, Mr. Halpern said, "Guess I'll get on my boots and go traipsing off, looking for him. He's probably scared stiff. And his mother hasn't helped any." He gazed thoughtfully at Crista. "Do you have any idea where he would go?"

Crista thought of the island, but Jeff didn't have his skates. And the ice wasn't as strong out in the middle. He knew that. Still, he could have gone up the point or into the woods. And then with a jarring crackle of fear, it hit her. Thunder!

"Oh, no!" Crista said, covering her mouth. "Oh, no!"

"What is it?" Mr. Halpern asked worriedly, peering into her eyes.

She shook her head. "Look down at the beach and up toward the point. I'll go into the woods."

"Do you know where he could be, Crista?" Mr. Halpern's voice was firm with authority.

She knew she couldn't hide it from him. "Jeff said something a few days ago that I just remembered."

"What?"

Both grandparents stepped closer into the cold air.

"The horses we've been riding at the Wilkins' farm. Jeff said he wished sometimes he could just disappear and ride away on Thunder, one of the horses."

"Let's get my car, Honey," Mr. Halpern said to his wife. Then he turned to Crista, "Can you show us how to get there?"

"Of course."

It was a flurry of activity for the next few minutes as both adults dressed for the cold. In five minutes everyone was sitting in Mr. Halpern's Oldsmobile and the engine jolted into reverse as he backed out into Rock Road.

"Up to the highway and down about a minute, I think," Crista said, not sure of distances.

"Would he really steal the horse?" Mrs. Halpern asked nervously.

"Mr. Wilkins would probably just let Jeff take him," Crista said. "He's very nice and Jeff knows how to saddle Thunder and everything."

They turned onto the highway and, in no time it seemed, they came to the sign to the Wilkins farm. Mr. Halpern swung to the right onto the road. Then, just as he stepped on the gas, Crista saw movement through the trees around the bend.

A second later, Jeff came into view. He sat forward on Thunder, galloping, roaring down the rutted road toward the car.

Mrs. Halpern screamed. Mr. Halpern opened his window. Crista jumped out the opposite side.

"Jeff!"

He was huddled over the horse's head in classic racing fashion. He didn't even stop as he went by. Crista shouted again, "Jeff! Stop! It's all right!"

But he had already reached the highway. Without even a look each way, the horse bolted across and both disappeared down the road on the other side.

"What is he doing?" Mr. Halpern screamed to Crista, still standing on the other side of the car and staring.

"I don't know!" she yelled back.

Suddenly both were aware of another roaring sound coming down the road. It was Mr. Wilkins in the Jeep. A second later he stopped.

"What is going on?" Mr. Wilkins roared, glancing at Mr. Halpern and then turning to Crista. "Jeff just took off like a bolt of lightning! And that horse has been crazy all morning!"

Crista quickly made introductions. "Jeff's scared because he saw the sheriff's car and thought he was going to be arrested."

Mr. Wilkins muttered something, then said, "Get in if you're going with me. If they get down to the lake I don't know what that horse will do. Remember the last time Thunder headed for the lake?"

Crista jumped into the Jeep. Mr. Halpern said, "I'll follow you."

Mr. Wilkins pulled up and waited as Mr. Halpern turned around. Then they both sped across the highway.

"Just when there's a thaw!" Mr. Wilkins yelled. "If Thunder gets out on the ice with that boy, they're both finished."

"Finished?" Crista yelled over the wind, unsure of what he meant.

"The deep six," Mr. Wilkins shouted, "drowning."

Crista's heart seemed to freeze inside and then with tearing eyes she prayed like she had never prayed before in her life.

·20·

Crazy Horse

The Jeep skidded and clunked along the road at high speed. There was still no sign of Jeff or Thunder. At this point, they couldn't be sure exactly where they went. Crista had no idea if they might have cut left or right onto one of the smaller roads through the woods. Mr. Wilkins was obviously following the fresh hoof marks as best he could, but a lot of snow had melted and the road was relatively clear.

They slowed down as they neared each cutoff, but the tracks continued to go straight ahead.

Then they saw him. Jeff lay in a crumpled heap on the side of the road, head first in a snowdrift. Jeff had been thrown from the horse's back! The Jeep crunched to a stop and Mr. Wilkins and Crista both jumped out.

Mr. Wilkins grabbed Jeff by the belt and pulled him out of the drift. He and Crista rolled him over. Jeff was unconscious. Mr. and Mrs. Halpern bounded out of their car behind the Jeep and ran up.

"Rub some snow on his face," Mr. Wilkins said.

Crista seized a handful from the drift and touched it to Jeff's cheeks. He twitched and blinked. Then he was crying. "I'm sorry, I'm really sorry. I . . ."

"It's all right," Mr. Wilkins cried. "Is anything broken?"

"No, I don't think so." Jeff started to stand. Crista and Mr. Wilkins gave him a hand and he rose to his feet. "Yeah, I'm okay, but I never should have taken Thunder, Mr. Wilkins. I'm sorry . . . I'm sorry."

Mr. Wilkins shook his head. "Don't worry about it. From what Crista tells me you've been under the gun lately, so let's just find Thunder and go home. Which way did he go?"

"Straight down the road," Jeff said. "I couldn't control him once he got going. It was like . . ."

"The horse has cabin fever or something again. I don't know what it is." Mr. Wilkins sighed. "I just hope he doesn't go for the lake. Let's get in the Jeep; we can still see his tracks."

Jeff hopped into the back of the Jeep and Crista took the right seat. Jeff's grandparents returned to their car and followed. With gravel and snow spitting out the back, Mr. Wilkins wheeled the Jeep forward. Crista turned to Jeff. He was still upset and crying.

"It's okay," she said to him. "The sheriff thinks Mrs. Holmes is an old crab and they're sure you didn't do anything."

"But I stole Thunder."

"Borrowed him for a ride," Mr. Wilkins said goodnaturedly. "You weren't going to do anything but calm down."

"But what if . . ."

"No what ifs," Mr. Wilkins shouted. "It'll work out. Just hang in there. The Good Lord isn't through with Thunder or any of the rest of us yet."

They churned and sidewinded down the road, snow, dirt, and sparks flying. In less than a minute, they reached Rock Road. Thunder appeared to have slowed, then turned in the direction of the access road to the lake. Mr. Wilkins shook his head. "That horse is plumb nuts."

He floored it, and everyone almost pitched out of the Jeep as they hit a big bump just over the lip of the windy path down from Rock Road. Mr. Halpern didn't follow, but stopped his car and Crista saw him open his door.

"Your grandparents will have to walk," Crista yelled.

Mr. Wilkins said, "It's all right. They might need a breath of fresh, horse-lathered air."

They shot onto the flat bit of road just before the beach. Then as they came out onto it and saw the lake, their worst fears were realized. Thunder stood on the ice, walking slowly across the lake. He still wore the saddle. He stood regal and proud, and apparently unaware of the danger that lay ahead.

"We've got to move fast," Mr. Wilkins said, jumping out. Crista and Jeff were right behind him.

"Thunder!" Mr. Wilkins called. "Whoa, boy!"

A moment later, there was a loud crack of ice.

Thunder disappeared in a shower of ice, water, and a high-pitched whinny of terror.

All three of them shrieked with horror—but it was too late.

"We can never get him out in time," Mr. Wilkins wailed. "Never."

Crista glanced at Jeff. His face was a stabbing throb of pain.

Mr. Wilkins stepped out onto the ice. Thunder bobbed up to the surface—he had opened a large hole. Fortunately he hadn't gone under so far that he would have ended up under the ice.

"Grab the rope," Mr. Wilkins yelled to Jeff as he walked out. Jeff ran back to the Jeep. Crista cautiously slid out next to Mr. Wilkins.

"What can we do?" Crista asked.

"Tie the rope on the pommel and try to pull him out," Mr. Wilkins answered. "That's all we can do. Problem is the ice might keep breaking, and we have to pull Thunder up and then across. A horse like that weighs over half a ton."

"We might break through, too."

"No, we should be able to get pretty close. Catching the pommel is what I'm worried about."

Jeff ran up with the rope. Mr. and Mrs. Halpern arrived on the beach and stood waiting. Mr. Halpern called out, "Is there anything I can do?"

"Pray!" yelled Mr. Wilkins. "You too," he said to Crista and Jeff. "This isn't going to be easy."

Twenty feet from the hole, Mr. Wilkins knelt. Thunder thrashed in the hole, his terrified eyes were wide open. One hoof pawed at the ice, which broke under the impact. The saddle rolled behind him as the horse pitched and neighed in the cold.

"How the heck can I do this?" Mr. Wilkins said, mostly to himself.

"I'll do it," Jeff said. "I should."

"How?" Mr. Wilkins asked, looking at him skeptically.

"I'm lighter and I can get up really close. If I can get it on the pommel and tie it ... "

"Not the pommel," said Mr. Wilkins. "The saddle has an opening just below the pommel on both sides. We've got to thread the rope through it."

"I can do it!" Jeff said fervently.

Mr. Wilkins studied his face. "Okay, maybe it'll work. Just don't fall in."

Jeff nodded.

"Let's tie one rope around your waist," Mr. Wilkins said. "Be careful."

He quickly cut the rope in two with his penknife, then cinched it around Jeff's waist. Then he gave him the other piece.

"Don't be a hero," Mr. Wilkins said as Jeff crept out toward Thunder. In a moment Jeff was prone, crawling on his elbows and knees toward the hole. Thunder whinnied and jabbed at the ice with his hoofs. Crista knew that in five or ten more minutes it would be too late. If they got Thunder out, he could die of hypothermia or any number of other illnesses.

Mr. Wilkins stood, yelling directions. Crista watched helplessly as Jeff neared the thrashing horse. She prayed again, then focused her mind on what they could do once the rope was around the saddle.

She saw Mr. Halpern walk out onto the ice behind them. When he reached them, he knelt by Mr. Wilkins. "Think we can pull him out?"

"I don't know," Mr. Wilkins answered, still staring at Jeff and Thunder. "All we can do is try."

The horse was still frenzied, but Jeff had reached the hole without breaking through. Crista prayed that somehow he'd get the rope threaded through the hole. Jeff leaned out. His jacket was soaked in a moment, as Thunder threw sheets of water up in his terror.

"Go!" shouted Mr. Wilkins. "You've got it."

Jeff was still way out on the ice. His face ducked into the water several times and he jerked off his ski cap and threw it further back on the ice.

"I should help," Crista said.

"No, stay here," Mr. Wilkins ordered, "we don't have another rope to tie to you."

Crista waited, her heart pounding like a drum roll.

Then Jeff shouted, "I've got it!" A cheer came up from Crista's throat. Jeff quickly knotted the rope and moved back. "Start pulling," he yelled.

Everyone stood and began to pull. But they couldn't get a grip on the ice. They kept slipping. "I should have thought of this," Mr. Wilkins yelled. "It'll never work!"

They all slid around, trying to get a foothold on the ice—but nothing would grip. The horse was lodged too low in the water. They couldn't get him up over the edge. It was hopeless. Thunder was a goner.

Then suddenly Crista remembered the dock. Things clicked into place—*yes, it could work.*

·21·

The Dock Trick

"Jeff!" Crista yelled. "The way you bring in your dock. With the fork and everything. Would that work? And you have longer rope."

"What's that?" Mr. Wilkins said, sweating. Jeff's lips were blue.

His teeth chattering, Jeff looked at his grandfather. "Granddad, it would work, wouldn't it?" Jeff said questioningly. His arms were shaking and his body looked like a goose pimple. "It will!" Jeff suddenly shouted. "Let's go!"

"What?" Mr. Wilkins yelled again.

"Get the Jeep turned around!" Mr. Halpern called as he ran in toward shore. "It might just work."

In moments, the Halpers and Crista were at the box on the Halpern property. Jeff grabbed the long fork and pulley from under the box and Mr. Halpern lifted out the rope. They sped back to the lake. Mr. Wilkins already had the Jeep turned around. As Jeff's granddad wrapped the rope around the trailer ball in the back, Jeff sped out onto the ice with the fork-pulley and tied the two ropes together—the one connected to Thunder and the longer rope from the box. It was a perfect square knot.

Crista cried, "What should I do?"

167

"Help me get the fork into the ice so it doesn't slide. Then get the rope up over it. We can't get too close, but we have to be close enough for Thunder to be lifted."

With the two ropes tied and retied, Jeff and Crista crept out to within 10 feet of Thunder. The horse was already subdued, as if he had given up.

"Don't give up, Thunder," Jeff said soothingly, "we're going to get you out. I promise."

Jeff chopped a pivot hole in the ice with the sharp end of the pole. Then he showed Crista how to drape the rope over the pulley. The rope was up a good 10 feet in the air. Mr. Halpern rushed out to stand with them, and yelled, "Hit it, Mr. Wilkins!"

Tires spun on the snow, but the Jeep quickly dug in and the rope tightened. There was a thrust and Jeff, Crista, and Mr. Halpern angled the fork for maximum lift. Thunder's saddle jerked the horse to the left, but suddenly, as the Jeep burned at the sand underneath the snow, Thunder started to rise.

"He's coming out!" Crista yelled. All three of them grabbed the pole to keep it in place.

"Keep going!" Jeff called to Mr. Wilkins.

Thunder's hooves clattered on the ice by the hole as his head and shoulders came out of the water. The pole moved backwards—toward the Jeep. Jeff, Crista, and Mr. Halpern leaned against it to keep it from going over.

"Push hard," Jeff cried.

Crista and Mr. Halpern leaned into it.

Then with a rush, Thunder blew out of the ice like a rocket. The pole came over and everyone leaped out of the way as the Jeep dragged Thunder sideways away from the hole.

Seconds later, Jeff called, "Ho! Stop!"

Mr. Wilkins turned around and stopped immediately. Then Thunder tried to get up. But he was
numb...he couldn't move.

Mrs. Halpern ran out with five blankets in her arms.

Grabbing one of them from his grandmother, Jeff
said, "Let's put the blanket under him and drag him in
all the way. He can't get up on the ice."

As the horse worked at rolling onto his feet, Crista
and Jeff draped a blanket into the spot vacated momentarily by the thrashing body. The moment it was
under him, Mr. Halpern shouted, "Hit it again. Drag
him out."

Mr. Wilkins didn't wait. With a sudden spraying of
stones and snow, the Jeep cranked forward, dragging
the horse all the way to the edge of the lake and up onto
the beach. Everyone ran after him, but Jeff's grandmother thrust a blanket over Jeff's shoulders. "Take
off your jacket," she said. "It's soaked. This will be
warmer."

Jeff's lips were nearly blue and he was still shaking
with whole body tremors, his lips and teeth chattering
like an angry squirrel.

Once on the beach, Thunder got onto his feet and
shook himself. Mr. Wilkins quickly untied the rope.
"I've got to get him into a warm stall as soon as pos-
sible."

"Can he walk?" Mr. Halpern asked.

"Run is more like it," Mr. Wilkins said with a tired
smile. "The next few days will tell if he'll survive." He
looked at Jeff. "Smart shootin' there, fella. You saved
the day."

Jeff nodded and motioned to Crista. "I-I-I-I-It w-w-
w-was Cr-Cr-Crista's idea." His body was shaking so
badly he couldn't get the words out.

"Talk later. Get up to the house," Mr. Wilkins answered. "Crista, can you help me get Thunder up the hill?"

Crista helped Mr. Wilkins pull the wet saddle and blanket off the shaking horse. Then he wrapped all four of the blankets Jeff's grandmother had brought from the house around Thunder, covering him as best as he could.

Then Mrs. Halpern led Jeff toward home. He was coughing now and his nose was running. "You're jumping into a hot tub, young man!"

Jeff nodded, glanced at Crista and Mr. Wilkins, and, still shaking all over, began following her meekly up the trail.

Mr. Halpern asked, "Can I do anything?"

"Just get the boy warm," Mr. Wilkins answered as he tied the bridle to the back of the Jeep. "Now, let's get this little no-good crazy stallion home." He swung up into the Jeep and Crista climbed in next to him.

He started up the path slowly, giving Thunder a chance to get his legs back. Thunder proceeded slowly. His eyes were blinking and he looked like he was about to fall asleep. Mr. Wilkins kept up a steady talk of encouragement. "Keep going, boy. Stay awake. We'll get there. Let's go."

Crista prayed again that Thunder would be all right.

Twenty minutes later they guided Thunder into the barn and his stall. Mrs. Wilkins was standing out in the yard waiting. "I'm going to rub him down," Mr. Wilkins said to her. "Go in the house and call the vet. Emergency."

As Mrs. Wilkins ran to the back door, Crista and Mr. Wilkins rubbed down the shivering horse. "It's going to be a battle," he said. "But I think—I hope—I pray—we make it. I'll take you home once the vet gets here."

"No rush," said Crista, her emotions spilling into her eyes. She was crying now and Mr. Wilkins came around the side and hugged her. "It's okay, Crista. Jeff is sorry and that's all I can ask. Things like this happen and all you can do is try to right them as best you can and leave the rest in God's hands."

"I know, but I never should have left him at the dock alone."

"You did what you had to do."

She nodded and continued brushing down the horse. She prayed that Jeff was already in a warm bed and that tomorrow everything would be better.

·22·

Friends

After examining Jeff, who was under an oxygen tent in the hospital, Dr. Mayfield told Mr. and Mrs. Halpern and Crista that it would be a matter of rest, antibiotics, and Jeff's commitment to listening and following the doctor's orders. He had double pneumonia. Jeff's mother had driven up immediately after she learned of the accident.

Thunder was also laid up, but the vet had been giving the horse shots and by the end of the week, he seemed to be out of danger. Every night Crista prayed for Jeff. She believed God could work miracles, and she was sure that nothing worse would happen. But it was hard waiting.

After two weeks of school and many visits to the hospital by friends, Jeff was sitting up, no longer coughing or in an oxygen tent, his green eyes cool, looking ready to joke around. Crista and Dr. Mayfield had come by that evening and Crista definitely wanted to surprise Jeff with something she had cut out of the newspaper the day before. Jeff's grandparents and mother were also in the room.

After the usual small talk, Crista pulled it out. The headline read: "More Break-Ins; Police Closing In."

Jeff gazed at it, not knowing what it meant.

"While you were in the hospital, there were four more break-ins!" Crista exclaimed. "So it proves it wasn't you once and for all—at least to everyone who seemed to be doubting you."

Jeff grinned. "Hey, that really is great news."

"Furthermore," Dr. Mayfield said, "Thunder's fine and Mr. Wilkins wants you over for a ride first thing. They'll be by again tonight, so don't go to sleep before seven-thirty."

The Wilkins' had come by twice in the previous weeks, but each time Jeff had been asleep and they hadn't wanted to waken him.

"So I guess it all worked out okay," Jeff said. There was still a hint of despair in his voice. Glancing at his mother, he said with regret, "I guess nothing will make dad show up."

His mother took Jeff's hand. "Honey, you've got to realize I love you and want you. I know I've been terrible lately, but this divorce took a toll on me, too. I'm sorry. I've been blaming you about everything."

Jeff nodded. "It's okay."

"No, it isn't okay," Mr. Wilkins said, stepping into the room with a huge grin. "But it's survivable."

He and Mrs. Wilkins were pushing a cart with something big on it, covered by a sheet.

"Mr. Wilkins, I'm so sorry..."

"Forget it," Mr. Wilkins said. "You were forgiven long ago. And just to prove it—" He ripped off the sheet. It was a shiny new western saddle. On the right-hand side were Jeff's initials, J.P.

"It's for you. We got one for Crista, too," Mr. Wilkins said. "As long as you're going to keep riding, you might as well have your own gear."

Jeff's chin had dropped and tears welled up in his eyes. He leaned forward and gave Crista a hug. "I guess it's not what you don't have that counts, but what you do have," he said as he looked around at everyone. "And I have some of the best friends ever."

Everyone was smiling and thanking Rollie and Carol for their gifts. But beneath the din, Jeff looked at Crista and said, "Thanks."

"For what?"

"For sticking with me. You're the first one."

"The first of many," Crista said. "Now get well. We have riding to do."

Other Good
Harvest House Reading

THE CRISTA CHRONICLES *Series*

Secrets of Moonlight Mountain

When an unexpected blizzard traps Crista on Moonlight Mountain with a young couple in need of a doctor, Crista must brave the storm and the dark to get her physician father. An exciting story of friendship and courage that draws Crista and her dad together.

Veteran youth writer Mark Littleton combines action and personal adventure with encouraging spiritual truth in contemporary stories that appeal to a broad range of middle-schoolers (age 9-13).

IN SEARCH OF RIGHTEOUS RADICALS
by *Sandy Silverthorne*

Kids use clues within each of the 14 stories to guess who the main character is. Highlights Bible characters who were radical enough to step out in faith when things seemed impossible—people like Elijah, Nehemiah, Peter, and Ruth. A one-sentence wrap-up woven into each story reinforces the important lesson kids learn from their Bible heroes.